she loves me

she loves me

Translated by Judith Sollosy

Péter Esterházy

hydra
books

NORTHWESTERN UNIVERSITY PRESS

EVANSTON, ILLINOIS

Hydra Books
Northwestern University Press
Evanston, Illinois 60208-4210

Originally published 1996 in Hungarian under the title
Egy Nö by Magvetö, Budapest. Copyright © 1996 by
Residenz Verlag, Salzburg and Vienna. English transla-
tion copyright © 1997 by Judith Sollosy. First published
in English in 1997 by Quartet Books Limited, London.
Hydra Books/Northwestern University Press edition
published 1997 by arrangement with Quartet Books
Limited. All rights reserved.

Printed in the United States of America

ISBN 0-8101-1557-3

Library of Congress Cataloging-in-Publication Data

Esterházy, Péter, 1950–
   [Egy Nö. English]
   She loves me / Péter Esterházy ; translated by
Judith Sollosy.
     p. cm.
   ISBN 0-8101-1557-3 (cloth : alk. paper)
   I. Sollosy, Judith. II. Title.
PH3241.E85N613 1997
894'.511334—dc21
                            97-28223
                              CIP

The paper used in this publication meets the minimum
requirements of the American National Standard for
Information Sciences—Permanence of Paper for
Printed Library Materials, ANSI Z39.48-1984.

she Loves me... **1**

There's this woman. She loves me.

she loves me...**2**

There's this woman. She hates me. Shadow. She calls me Shadow. For instance: so you're here again, Shadow? she'll ask, hanging about? At other times: it's stuffed cabbage for lunch, Shadow, you mind? Or playfully: I'm casting my Shadow before me, by which she means *me*, it's a reference to me, and it's supposed to mean that I'm asking for big trouble. However, this playful abandon does not necessarily mean she's in high spirits, though when she is in high spirits, she sometimes hoots merrily: Shadow world! which, like it or not, is yet another reference to yours truly. On the other hand, when her spirits are low, when her older sister calls from Lübeck, for instance, or when she takes it into her head she's gained too much weight, though I swear to high heaven that I could just *die* for every ounce of her living flesh, she'll declare that I am the tree that keeps her from seeing the forest.

I won't leave her side, no matter what. When she opens

her mouth, gaping *ah-ah-ah-ah!* I open my mouth, too. When she sits down, I curl up by her side like a puppy. When she passes out, breathless, I go and ask someone to fetch the smelling salts. She lowers her lashes and an almost imperceptible tremor runs through me. When she lifts her arm, it's like I am exercising, too. If a convenient bit of wall space presents itself, she makes a bunny rabbit, dog or eagle for the kids. At such times I, too, am a bunny rabbit, dog or eagle. I want her, but my progress is fraught with difficulty, to say the least. It advances by fits and starts. Sometimes I'm *that close*, at others we're light-years apart. Not that it makes a difference, for I must dance to her tune – around, in front of, under and behind her. There's a certain ebb and flow to our affairs. What the hell is that supposed to mean, Shadow? she explodes, because if she so much as suspects I want her, if she gets *wind* of my desire, it's like oil on troubled waters. Instead of fanning her flame, my wanting her makes her settle into a comfortable sense of ownership.

Sometimes she cannot talk to me openly. (The reasons vary from the political to her situation at work, from the logistics of public transportation to domestic affairs. Her father hates my guts and refers to my work as shadow play, or shadow-boxing. He also says that I'm my own darker, shadowy side, not to mention the fact that I cast a shadow over his daughter's life, and the like. A narrow-minded old goose is what *I'd* like to say, if only he weren't such a lovable old chap notwithstanding, substantial and attractive. A handsome, grey-haired *male*.) At such times she puts an edge to her voice in order not to give herself away, and talks to me with such grating indifference, my heart skips a beat. I am scared to death I might lose her and would do anything she asked, anything at all. Is that so? Would you even bring me flowers? Of course, that wouldn't be you, Shadow, you'd never bring me flowers. You'd rather break your wrist. And she nods knowingly. After a bit of reflection

I say she's right, you're right, honeybunch, but afterwards, with my hand in a cast, I'd bring you those flowers all the same. I'd carry them pressed to my stomach, and big flowers only. Big hulky flowers so they won't slip out between the cast and my stomach, such as gladioli, yes, mostly gladioli. I'd go for gladioli in a big way. Just think what it would do for the gladioli business. Mmm. Gladioli. Yes, my one and only. Gladioli.

The gladioli make her tremble in the balance, and she wants me. She stands in front of the wall like a condemned man, taking advantage of the backlighting; she approaches me slowly, standing firm in her decision; she stops, I stop; there is no turning back now; she rubs it, she is covered in plaster, insulating plaster (perlite), white, like the face of a clown. She trembles, she pants. I hardly dare stir. What do you expect me to say now? That the members of the firing squad, men and women both, stand ready, their guns cocked? Or that their faces are white, too, perlite-white, like the face of a clown?

she loves me...**3**

There's this woman. She hates me. She wants me. She calls all the time. And leaves messages. She's even bought an Ansaphone so she can leave me messages. She's a busy lady who never calls from the same place twice. I'm not at liberty to talk now, she whispers into the phone. Then next time she calls, she explains why not. (The reasons vary.) Then when we meet, she explains her calls. The bathroom throbs with excitement, AT&T and long distance, she giggles furtively, she's in *sneaking* good humour.

There's this woman. She loves me. She calls and says my name. Month after month, she repeats my name like some magic formula. I wonder when she sleeps. My party line must be up the wall, except they won't complain to the phone company because sometimes they can listen in on our 'conversation'. Meanwhile, the snows of yesteryear have melted, the muddy puddles have dried up, the trees are in bloom, you can buy green peppers not grown in hothouses, though individually only, to be sure; fungus appears in the moist parts and cavities of the body, Parliament has just ratified the second Jewish laws (it being 3 May 1939), and Ludwig von Baden, Jr., has also ousted the Turks from the country.[1] In the space of ten seconds she manages to say my name a dozen times, though in the long run this figure is not wholly accurate, for

---

[1] Ludwig von Baden helped to oust the Turks from Hungary in 1686.

periodically she takes a sip of water. I have so far refrained from talking into the phone. I am afraid she might go into shock. Or, who knows, maybe she's got the wrong number.

There's this woman. She loves me. She's got this thing about the past, though, especially the individual's and the community's, her own and the nation's. She can't resign herself. For instance, she won't accept Hungary's surrender at Világos.[2] If only that General Dembinsky had had a wee bit more brains stuck inside his head. Or why couldn't Kossuth *love* Görgey? Have you any idea, Mister, what an ass I had? No, of course not. How could you?! And don't go thinking of an ass like a mare's, mind you, a classical baroque *swirl*, not that sort of admittedly pleasing triviality. You, Mister, see only what *is*. On 18 February 1853, the tailor's apprentice János Libényi

---

[2]General Dembinsky led the Hungarian forces. In the losing battle, it fell to Görgey, who had favoured a compromise with the House of Habsburg all along, to lay down arms. Needless to say, the great statesman and fighter for Hungary's independence, Louis Kossuth, was not pleased with Görgey's capitulation.

attempted to assassinate the Emperor. But all *you* see is that it's sagging, that my ass is on its way down.

She likes kissing (re: Kossuth–Görgey), she *gushes* with good cheer, she laughs, she giggles, she whinnies – these being types of kisses. What fun! she chuckles inside my mouth, more, come on, hey, just a little more; her tongue stiffens, it practically knocks against the roof of my mouth, warbling in the depths, in the darkness that is mine. You, Madame, are the Paganini of the kiss, I say, awed. Shut up! I'm busy! Kisses crawl all over her, over the suntanned curve of the neck, the cheeks, the nose, the sockets of the eyes; there are kisses in her glance, too, the temples, the top of the head; the thighs stir, more like a quiver, touch and part, and the ribs and the bones . . .

The surrender at Majtény,[3] she whispers.

---

[3]Majtény: another battle, another loss, this one in 1711, during the wars for freedom headed by Prince Rákóczy II.

There's this woman. She hates me. She's got bad breath. A variety of odours issue from her mouth. These can be classified into two main groups: to wit, when she has eaten, and when she has not. The identification of the former is a fun-filled, though admittedly inconsequential, undertaking – cauliflower soup, cabbage with pork, not to mention those *saftig* gourmet touches, onion and garlic. On the other hand, scallions in her salad call for a certain forbearance. And we're talking about a hygienic woman here, all this being disguised by the brushing of teeth, not infrequently accompanied by mouthwash.

It's when she hasn't eaten that matters take a more serious turn. At such times there is no yesterday and there is no sunset when a certain someone had eaten, no, *this* does not exist, and there is no time, and no cause and effect, there is no *logic*, no history, no remembrance of things past (and consequently, no morals), and there is no society either –

10

not to mention the country, the homeland and the nation. There is just one person from whom (I know her, that's why I say what I say) the impersonal issues forth in the shape of a lukewarm, putrid stink.

But no, its not a stink, it's less, which makes it all the more disturbing, a light nothing of a smell, exceedingly and excessively insufficient. If only I didn't love kissing her more than anything, I'd never even notice. If only a nagging, incessant need for her didn't compel me to seek out her lips, I wouldn't even know about this blemish, this sore at the heart of creation, this open outrage. The whole woman − it's like a light breeze blowing from the glue factory. But the gentleness is the hardest to bear, when I cover her face with a series of little short kisses, or pecks, when I kiss her eyes, her lids, her eyeballs, nose, ears, cheeks, temples, and − by definition − her lips and her mouth too, alas! This is so repulsive, and I attain such wild peaks of disgust, that it makes my head reel. On the other hand, the more frenzied, insentient and brutal I am, in short, when − let's not mince words − I fall on her like an animal, practically biting her lips out of her as if we were wolfing each other down, chins snapping, tongues flapping, and there's taste of blood, the less I have to think of the glue factory − which, by the way, has just been privatized for peanuts.

This is why, when I spot her in a place fit for kissing − and there is hardly any place left these days that private or social consensus, virtue or sobriety, has put under interdiction − I up and run at her, Speedy Gonzales, that's me! and *wham!*, I slam into her, we slam into each other with no time to spare, because I know only too well that otherwise this foul emptiness, this putrid absence of absence will overwhelm me, this fetid nothingness, this pestiferous air which, and this has been known to happen, makes me retch − snot and saliva running together − though this, too, is a form of *intercourse*, I guess.

11

And she knows this. That's why she hates me. It's reassuring, I swear. Of course she misconstrues the situation, thinking I'm doing it out of the goodness of my heart. That's why she hates me. Whereas that's not why, it's because I'm crazy for her. When I close my eyes I see only her, and when I open them, there is nothing I wouldn't do to see her. Once she realizes this, she's going to love me, too. Not that I really care. What I care about is that I shouldn't lose sight of her.

There's this woman. She loves me. If she's not Finnish, I'll eat my hat. At first, we even said, isn't it hunky-dory? We're *related*. 'Are you Finno-Ugrian, too, if you don't mind my asking?' We try to discover national traits in each other. Unfortunately, I'm not conversant, I'm not the least bit conversant with Finnish history (it's major mineral resources: chrome, titanium, cobalt, vanadium, copper, zinc and nickel) and have only the vaguest 'northern' images to go by, and so I hold on to these banalities like so many straws – my points of reference. I try to place her in some sort of context, stuff her inside some national cliché, but it's no good, because her real context is my body. Her homeland is not her homeland, my body is. When I look at her, trying to figure her out, it's not the image of the tablelands of Finland that I see, the abundant, cascading rivers as they surge forward between its lakes, but myself; I always see myself, too, my thighs, which we can safely call muscular, and at times the twitching muscles of my backside, the cheeks of my backside, or my moist lips, my finger.

For years and years she positively denied feeling the same way about me. But then, in the heat of an all-out knock-down fight, she finally came clean. 'I look at you,' she screeched, 'and all I see is my cunt! I see you in the shadow of my cunt!' I don't like her talking like that. I don't like her calling the parts of our bodies by their names without due reflection. For her part, she hates my silence. 'Now . . . now you're silent about your prick!' she says revealingly. 'And the cleft between my ass! What's the big deal?!' To me it *is* a big deal. But I say nothing. What could I say? The fact that she feels about the body, my body and her body, the same way I do is all the more surprising given the ease with which she knows her way around Hungarian affairs. She's got pronounced views on the battle of Vezekény ('it was neither as inconsequential nor as fruitless as it might first appear'); she uses the expression 'the Drágffy method', in reference to the brave warrior who, discarding his spurs, galloped to his death with the national flag at the ill-fated battle of Mohács; she's familiar with the anecdotes about Deák and Imre Nagy's 1953 reforms; she knows who were sentenced during the so-called minor-league, and who during the so-called major-league literary trials. She can even tell one Democratic Forum tendency from the other.[4]

---

[4]In short, the lady is on intimate terms with Hungarian history from the ill-fated battle of Mohács (1526), where King Louis II and his troops lost to the Turks, through the battle of Vezekény (1652), where four young Esterházys lost their lives fighting for the same cause; from the losing battles against the Habsburgs, culminating in the 1848–9 wars of independence, in which the reformer and politician Ferenc Deák was a motive force, through Imre Nagy, another reformer, though Communist, and though executed after the failed uprising of 1956. The Hungarian Democratic Forum came to power during more peaceful times, when the first post-Communist elections were held in 1990. (They have since failed to be re-elected.)

Our increasingly frequent and – to be perfectly frank and above-board – furious fights, which from time to time end in mutual assault, with me shaking her, sometimes by the neck, which in all fairness could be construed as strangling, with her showing a marked preference for throwing things, and not only books and plastic ashtrays but pictures, too, pulled off the wall or, more traditionally, vases, or, in a certain sense surprisingly, cast-iron meat grinders, though she has been known to opt for the silverware laid out on the table which, seeing as we were about to have Wiener schnitzel, included knives and could thus be regarded as assault with a deadly weapon – in short, our fights, I think, had nothing to do with our shared Finno-Ugrian roots. Or did they? Could it have been the nightmare of time spent together? The wandering, the hunting, the tending of the herd, the adoration of the self-same gods? Or the nightmare of recognition? After all, she's even familiar with my silences! Who knows, perhaps she even dreams about me . . . or I about her . . . What's the use of this sort of pitiful proximity? This sort of mirroring?

'I know what you're thinking!' she lashed out at me shrilly, 'that it would be better, better for us, if I were God. That's what you're thinking. But don't you think you're better. You're no better. No, sir! Because I think the same thing about you, that it would be better, better for us, if you were . . .'

This marshalling of the troops happened after the fucking battle of Vezekény. Words were of no avail, silence was of no avail, we just went round and round in circles. At times it is not worth it, trying to distinguish between love and hate, I have read somewhere. I find such sentences repugnant. And yet there was something to be said for it, some feeling had taken a hold on us, and there was no knowing where it would lead. Or trying to influence it. Or holding out hope. Our lovemaking, too, was different at the time, more frequent, desperate.

15

Once I told my father about this. What I mean is, I asked him what northern women were like. He shrugged and made a face. 'How should I know?' Still, he asked me to his room, where I hadn't been in a long time, and pointed to a painting which I had seen many times as a child, in another apartment, in another dark, dimly lit room, a ponderous, dromedary oil painting in an ornate, self-assertive, nineteenth-century frame. It depicted Norwegian fishmongers at the market by the sea. The wind was up and a mysterious light was pouring forth, and it was neither dark, nor light, nor nightfall. Dark and light and grey and bright, a bright darkness, a shimmering glow, eternal twilight. I had my eye glued to the painting, my father had his eye glued to me.

Standing in their wooden clogs, looking merry and intent, the fishmongers were throwing their fish about. To me they looked just like this Finnish woman. And their hips swayed with an indescribable strength and ease, with a *substantial* liveliness. Girls and women at the same time, pack-mules and Northern fairies, that's what they were, though their hips were good civilian hips, hard-working, of the body. I said goodbye to my father, and henceforth made this frame the Finnish woman's lodgings. I localized her there, this became her home. These many massive, monumental women. And now when I look at her I needn't see myself any more, not my thighs and not the twitching muscles of my backside, the cheeks of my backside, nor my wet lips, nor my finger, and I don't even have to think that it might be better, better for us, if she were . . . However, I won't even say it. Instead, teasing like two relatives, we go on asking each other, 'Are you Finno-Ugrian, too, if you don't mind my asking?'

There's this woman. She hates me. She loves me. For a whole afternoon she loved me. The word fuck I don't like, and the word lay I like even less; the word screw I like, but it doesn't like the text, it – if you'll pardon the expression – screws it up, while I can't be expected to sink so low as to say, in italics, of course: we're doing *it*. That would make me puke. If only the first person singular of the sentence were just a bit more removed from my person; if, in short, my sense of responsibility were not quite so acute, which would be great (we are working at it), I'd feel free, and, above all, I wouldn't feel the need to appear, even if only partially or ironically, in my best colours, then, to wit, if I were a romantic hero from head to toe, the bridge between 'I' and 'us' (to mention only the most important types of suspension bridges: the plain, the separately secured, self-secured, and also cable bridges, the slant-cable harp bridge, the slanted star-cabled, the slanted fan-shaped and the single-pillared

17

slanted harp–cabled) – well, in that case, above and beyond this well, I'd say that we spent the afternoon making whoopee.

It's not the abandon, the unbridled recklessness with which we fell on each other time and time again that I'd mention first, the way we crashed into each other, the basic and elemental nature of which no doubt bears a certain significance, nor the obvious fact that it felt good, it felt *ter-rific*, though this would bring us a step closer to what I want to talk about, the impersonal carnality, the wallowing in the carnality which is within us yet is basically independent of us, the pagan rejoicing of the body. We both ended up with sore muscles; my prick was on fire and her pussy was on fire, and we had to resort to the use of Vaseline, and we were gasping for breath as if we had just scaled the summit of a very high mountain (ex: the Patootiecatapetl). I put my arms around her, that's how I fell asleep, what I mean is, I fell asleep, and she snored, because she fell asleep, too, snoring in an airy sort of way, like the Finns, whereas she's as Magyar as Attila the Hun. Is this what I wanted to say? That she was sleeping in my arms innocent as a baby? No. On the contrary. What I mean is, explanations *of all sorts* are bad, while I still have something to say. For instance, it's true that she lay there gently and quietly, and me, with passions spent. I won't say happily, but not unhappily either. That goes without saying. Nor sadly (*post coitum* and what have you), as the Latin proverb would have us believe. Not satisfied, yet satiated. I lay there with that woman, with that woman in that room (for another five minutes or so, like in a banal comedy), so that there were no questions in me, nor were any questions forthcoming, either from Karelia in Finland or the Csallóköz in Transylvania, or His kingdom in the skies. There was nothing open to question about my life, my being, my position. This is what I wanted to say.

There's this woman. She loves me. She's a great lay. Fucks like an angel, though I'd be hard put to say why. (Or would I?) Why indeed? Who can explain it, who can tell you why? Other women have the same mastery over their muscles and the same ease about their licentiousness, an ease which instead of threatening you is infectious, nor does she enjoy a monopoly over the high spirits which come trickling from her every pore; others have a similar capacity to transform said high spirits with such surprising suddenness into something dramatic, tugging at it like an undertow, and which, through the pain, enhances the ecstasy. Still, as she sits comfortably atop me (I am lying on a cornflake!), or as I writhe helpless between 'the vice of her marble thighs' to the infinite rhythm of the seas, well, that's far out! All the time that we *are* there is nothing but this joy, this joy crowds everything else out, I cease to be, and she ceases to be, there is nothing but this elemental rejoicing. And so, I don't even have to think how it will all end soon, which is a blessing, because I'd rather die than have it end. The word joy is not even the right word. And the Lord saw that it was good, yes, that's the right word, good. (By the way, she questions all of this. *Flatly* denies it. No, she is not a bed-bunny, a numero uno hot potato, nor has anyone ever called her that, ever, and no wonder, and she can't figure what nonsense I'm talking about, a good thing it's not the pagan rejoicing of the body, or some such nonsense. One thing is certain, though. Her body seems to have changed lately. It is not any more supple or compliant, perhaps, but inquisitive, yes, her body has become more inquisitive, and this probing and prying, it is very much like wanting, yes, there's more wanting to her, which comes as a surprise to her, too, she says, but it's not something she knows, but something I bring out in her, my body, my body being the coin that's thrown into her to make her click, so that, old chum, without you I'm just a half-a . . . just a one-armed bandit in bed.)

she loves me... **10**

There's this woman. She hates me. She's after the ocean, the faint glimmer, the truculent light, neither dark nor light, the eternal twilight. And she won't let up until she gets her way. She likes it when the wind is up. I hate it. I hide behind her for shelter. And stay put until there is precious little left to worry about. How different this would be on dry land! A betrayal, she'd say, unworthy, she'd whine squeamishly, like animals, she'd hiss, an outrage against our bodies, she'd whisper softly, which I would find touching and romantic, and tell her, too, softly, touchingly and romantically, on dry land – but she's tugging at my trouser belt by then, practically ripping it off, whereas pulling down the zipper would suffice, silly gal, but I keep mum; besides, I'm busy; not to be checked, my finger forges ahead as if drawn by a magnet, *allons, enfants de la patrie!*, or the Pacific Ocean, meanwhile I feel my end approaching, I'm worried about my trousers, they're made of the finest material, I clap my free hand over myself, but

21

what does she care, but let bygones be bygones, and we stay like that for a moment, bent into a spasm, then disengaging ourselves we laugh, we laugh and chortle, like after some practical joke. We glance at the ocean and laugh, it shimmers and quivers and slides around, my ocean, it shimmers and quivers and slides around her blouse, my trousers, the stain, the Cossack ottoman.

There's this woman. She loves me. She's a nature freak and she prates on and on about the cosmos, the miracle of nature and the order and symmetry that can be discovered therein, and also the beauty that can be discovered within us as a consequence – in short, about 'the mutual embrace of the transient and the infinite', but she lets on that at such times she's really thinking of God, except she's loath to call Him by His name, and that it is easier to reach God by way of an oak tree or a dragonfly, that infinitesimal creature superior to the most intricate of machines, than ... than by attending church, not to mention scholastic literature. What the hell, I ask, has the oak tree got to do with scholastic literature? I don't get it. She shrugs. She's bright. Quick on the uptake. But explanations she does not like. For her something is either obvious, or it does not exist.

In summer she wears a pair of loose, wide, knee-length cotton culottes, beige, which emphasizes her strong thighs and backside, highlighting them, as it were. There is also amazing strength in her calves and her chest. I know them inside and out. She makes faces a lot, exaggerating her expressions like in the silent movies, and she squints from the bottom up. Her eyebrows are heavy, like some thicket, and are tweezed at the bridge of the nose. Won't the follicles get inflamed? At this she leaves me high and dry, hearing the thing about the follicles, she gives me the slip. Sometimes she even slaps me on the back, as if to encourage me. To do what, I wonder?

The rain doesn't phase her. I always walk hugging the wall, the hood pulled over my head; she goes bareheaded, and heads where she's got something to do. Yet around here, the rain doesn't even fall; it appears, it attacks, and not from above, either, but perfidiously, from the side. An umbrella is a foolish thing at such times, a thing of vanity, and whoever has one all the same, either because he is a foreigner, or because it is in his nature, wields it like a sabre, staggering round and round in circles: now from here? now from there? and now, from over here?! The Three Musketeers.

Mostly, it is she who calls the shots. (The first time was an exception, I forced her to take me in her mouth. Admittedly, she made a face, but I couldn't decide, was she play-acting, let's say, like in a silent film, or was she disgusted, or simply not up to it? Later on all this got mixed up with the ocean wind, the caprice of nature, and the cosmos, for whatever it's worth. It is also typical that when the time came, she didn't swallow it, but she didn't spit it out either, but ever so gently let it trickle back on to my stomach.)

The kind of landscape I like does not like man, it rejects him, there is no room for him there. A landscape before man. When you reach such a landscape, your imagination knows no bounds, you can imagine anything you like, you can think anything you want into this world, anything at

24

all. It is a landscape for which there are no similes. No wonder. There is no one to do the comparing. And she shrugs like a presumptuous youngster. She is constantly preoccupied with words and agonizes over them, especially how something can be described in words. For instance, no wonder, she says, that the Eskimos or whoever have some forty-odd words for snow. When she sees a waterfall, she's overcome by helpless outrage. Just look at this fucking waterfall! Wouldn't it be a lot more decent to shut up? Or do you expect me to list how it swirls and churns and hops and skips and jumps on the rocks head first, plunging to the depths, misting and eddying? Preposterous! she whined. And can't I see, it's like trying to catch a sparrow by beating on a drum. The minute a problem is put into words, it becomes incapable of a solution. Only a serendipitous discovery is a real discovery. Or, and she squinted at me, where there are a lot of waterfalls, there are a lot of waterfall words. In Hungary, what have we got a lot of in Hungary? And she started beating my chest, how humiliating, how embarrassing, what a wash-out! A fiasco! – and shaken to her foundations, she announced that the world cannot be described in words *after all*. When this happens, I keep my mouth shut (once I happened to mention Jókai's epic description of the lower reaches of the Danube.[5] You should have heard that screeching!), and plan ahead how we are going to make love soon, though it's good only when I don't plan ahead, and so, because I have no intention of thwarting this culture slut, I plan ways to make love to other women instead. If only I felt like it.

In short, when we are in the vicinity of a waterfall, she's up in arms, while I am woebegone. The grass stained her skirt but she didn't mind; before pulling on her panties, she

---

[5]Mór (Mauricius) Jókai's famous description of the 'Iron Gate' stretch of the Danube before it was regulated to allow maritime traffic can be found in his *Timar's Two Words* (*Az Aranyember*), 1873.

ran down to the river's edge, to the bottom of the waterfall, to splash it with water. Hey, she shouted to me from down there, what do you think, could each of us be a waterfall? And she flapped her skirt.

she loves me... **12**

There's this woman. She hates me. Her eyes are as grey as mine, and since mine are as grey as my mother's, when our eyes meet, it's like I've made it home. From a distance her body is like a girl's, from close up, like a clay pit. Her arms are heavy, her lips grainy, like raspberries. She bullies me all the time. Tells me not to worry (*Don't worry, be happy!*), she's fine, her health couldn't be better, she's *one hundred per cent OK*. And she slaps me on the back, like a mischievous child. Besides, she was born under a lucky star, she feels. After all, so many wonderful things happen to her. They come in droves. For instance? For instance, my face. The way it can whatchamacallit, beam. And that look of surprise! . . . And no man has ever said thank you to her, at least, not quite like this. But I mustn't take it to heart. I see only her lap, neither her heavy arms, nor her raspberry lips, nor the little-girl clay pit. *Pe-lease! Pe-lease!* I shriek, squeal, beg. Could that be what she has in mind? Could this *pe-lease* be my thank-you? And that her head's been spinning ever since, the world turning round with her, oh, so much ecstasy, so much abundance, and she can feel everything once again, like when she was a little girl, her body, it sings, it tingalings, it breaks into song, and can't I get it through my thick skull, it has opened up, like a flower. But I mustn't take it to heart.

There's this woman. She loves me. It's just that I must wait my turn. When we go out to dinner, there are always six or seven other men besides me. (There are always seven men besides me, always the same seven men, even the one whose younger brother committed suicide recently is with us; in the morning he went shopping, mailed some letters – no farewell letters, though – then jumped out of the window. Tenth storey. Pre-fab housing.) They're adorable. The woman thinks so too. (For the sake of the truth, this is *her* opinion. I merely share it.) She has a way of sneaking up on me and whispering in my ear, 'Look! Aren't they adorable?' She's proud. They are the apple of her eye.

We go to the best restaurants, especially fish places. We eat fish three, more often four times out of every five. We prefer salt-water fish to fresh-water fish, Serbian carp being the one exception. Serbian carp is everybody's special favourite.

I am always the last and must wait my turn, wait and wait and wait. You'd think the night would never end. Though sometimes it's the other way around, and it's as if someone might put an end to it at any time, abruptly, before my turn could come. Of course, I wait, if I can. At times it's the number zero that'll chill the heart, sometimes the infinite. At others, the double-digit twenty-eight. They all have an excuse for getting ahead of me. At times this makes me feel bad, at others it makes me feel special (warm-up bands and the like).

One member of our group happens to be a sailor. Danubian. But let that pass. He takes things in his stride. He laughs a lot, and from the heart. He likes to talk about his family, his two little girls and his wife, whose hair is done up in braids, two golden braids. Notwithstanding, he is refined and sensitive and knows how to tell an interesting tale. He throws in an impressive number of seafaring words and expressions, and gets a kick out of it ('If there's a blue patch the size of a sailor's pants hooked to the sky at eleven in the morning, there's gonna be sunshine that day'); he is easily offended ('My old man,' he told us, 'died of eating a mackerel that's been to Stockholm,' meaning it wasn't a fresh catch, but giggling was out, not to mention the fact that his father had never been further afield than Nyírbátor[6]); and he's got a good ear for vague hints. He is younger than I am, wide in the shoulder, muscular. I've only seen him in his heavy tweed jacket so far. It's how I imagine a young man should look. On the other hand, given half a chance, he won't stand on ceremony. When only three of us are left, which happens pretty often – he, myself and the woman – there's nothing he'd like better than to throw me out of the bar, because after dinner, we always do the town. There are two or three spots we visit, always in the same order,

[6]A town on the Great Hungarian Plain. But don't go looking for it in any encyclopaedia.

blues and rock and roll places, nostalgic, at which, given the fact that they are both younger than me, the sailor and the woman scowl something awful. The sailor won't mince his words. Once he said, 'I mean the world to her, and don't you forget it!' But he smiled. Sometimes he even squeezes my arm. A man who looks out for himself, that's for sure. 'Find a cab and get the fuck out of here!' I smile back and nod, 'Sure, sure, but not just yet,' and I go on nodding as if we were brothers.

I am surprised by my own determination and steadfastness of purpose. Because when all is said and done, this is what I have discovered, that I am steadfast and determined. Because that's not how it starts. At the start I'm more like a gatecrasher looking for a hand-out. For instance, I'll run my fingers over the exceptionally beautiful, and I imagine expensive, greenish-blue cashmere shawl (the woman's), and in the process my hand just happens to slip down her neck, at which she quickly turns her head, pressing the back of my hand against her collar-bone the way an adroit businessman or secretary does the telephone. At other times, though, at another time of the night, I am more like a fearless hunter, an experienced old shark who knows that time is on his side, *time is on my side, yes, it is!*, the wind, now it's blowing from here, and now from there, and now from over here, the thing to do is bide your time, lie low, and keep your eye on the prey. However, I make sure the sailor doesn't see everything. I'd feel silly, having him see right through me (especially as I blink idiotically, closing my lids over her). That would put me at a disadvantage.

These are long nights. Long. They drag on and on with mighty inner and outer contingencies, surprises and unexpected turns of event. But they always end the same way, thank God. (The other day the cocks started a scuffle. The sailor and I steered clear, but then he and the woman tried to break up the fray, and this was like they were in it, too; I could see them feeling the woman up, the sailor included. They ended up kissing three at the same time, on the cheek, or whatever. I was sitting on a bar stool. If one of them happened to glance my way, I could detect a touch of hatred in his eye. I can sit on a bar stool the way others sit in an easy chair, and that's something few men can honestly say for themselves.)

There's this woman. She hates me. Or I hate her, is that what I mean? In any case, when she sees me, be it in her bathroom as I squat miserably over her bidet, or in her kitchen as I spoon down the chicken soup which in the meantime has turned into jelly (basically, I'm chewing the wings), or when I'm helping her kids with their homework (right now we're preoccupied with the construction of triangles, though we've been known to have problems with quadratic equations and so-called open sentences, too, not to mention the discussion of inequalities and set theory in general, and the biology of the stag-beetle), or when I lie down in the back room for a short nap, and I do mean short because otherwise it's like being hit over the head and I can't seem to pull myself out of the murky depths of the afternoon, but also away from the house, in town, at major thoroughfare crossings, most especially at pedestrian crossings, or when standing in front of a shop window, longing for an etymological dictionary, or as I am self-importantly studying the menu displayed at a restaurant door, not to mention villages, cemetery fences and pheasant shoots – in short, wherever she sees me, in the bathroom, the kitchen, the hall, the back room, in town or country or by a cemetery fence or in the fields – she ups and seduces me.

She gives me a look with those bedroom eyes of hers. She closes her lids over me. Or her lips turn moist, and that's how. Her nostrils tremble like butterfly wings. She snorts like an animal. She wraps her seduction in colourful robes, the essence of each being flattery. She leads me to believe that (*a*) I am God's gift to women, and (*b*) if for any reason I am not, she still gets the hots for me. She breaks out in a sweat. Her knees buckle. Her tongue gets tied. She can't live without me. She needs me. I must help. It's no skin off my back, that's obvious. Given the slightest provocation, she'll cross her legs, at which her skirt hikes up to mid-thigh, while my eyes – to use a hackneyed expression – practically pop out of their sockets. Which she'll subtly acknowledge. But subtlety is not the sole trademark of her seduction. By way of example let me just mention her habit of showing up out of the blue, pushing me against the wall like a man, forcing my legs apart with her knee, this being by the post office, next to the red letter box as, unsuspecting, I am about to post a letter, or, on the contrary, she'll kneel humbly in front of me, waiting until the last postcard or letter has disappeared through the slot, then she'll peel me out of my pants and, sometimes cheerfully, sometimes in deadly earnest, ominously, you might say, she'll busy herself with me. She'll play with me, or else *get down* to business. Sometimes she won't talk to me the whole day, preferring to flirt with complete strangers, coming on, then demurring, but she's not obvious about it, it's not blatantly against me, with her stabbing me, in this negative manner, to the quick with a smile, making me the lead character of the story, of *her* story, oh no. She's completely oblivious to my presence. But then, when I least expect it, well into the night, be it in the bathroom, or in town, or in the country, she'll turn to me in humble supplication: sleep at our place, please. The night is fragile, the silence profound, with this request only hovering in the untroubled dark: sleep at our place, please.

But she can't seduce me all the time. Twice already she couldn't seduce me. One time I was too sleepy; the other I can't recall (possibly I didn't want her enough, preferring to watch TV), but both times I was so filled with infantile pride I couldn't wait to call her back, begging her for visiting rights. To which she magnanimously consented.

In short, she picks me up every chance she gets. She has her way with me. What this means to her I can't think through to its logical conclusion. But she makes my life complete. On Tuesday I went to Nyíregyháza.[7] I had an errand to run for my sister. I stayed in the dorm which – how shall I put it? – was permeated with the air of the Kádár era, and some unsavoury chemical stench thrown in for good measure. I find a note on my bed: call Room 404 right away. Ring twice, then put the phone down, this being the signal, because she's not alone, but would then come and drop by ('for a quickie'). There is no Room 404 at Nyíregyháza, and there is no phone, which is an example of the completeness I'm talking about.

Though I'm no fieldmouse on the lookout for its fated falcon, wherever I am, be it over the bidet or on a pheasant shoot, I am waiting for her to pounce on me. When we run into each other afterwards she doesn't bat an eyelid, and then I haven't said the half of it. Despite the fact that *pro forma* it's always me getting the short end of the stick, I am always in a blue funk lest I humiliate her. For instance, in Nyíregyháza we wound up having a convivial dinner.

---

[7]Appreciably larger than Nyírbátor, but don't go looking, etc., etc.

Who the fuck do you think you're fucking with!, this, too,
I am quite capable of thinking.

There's this woman. She loves me. She keeps trying to put my mind at ease. For instance, I swear to you, she'll say, I don't hate you one bit. Then, all choked up, she'll add: and now I'm off on my bike, before I explode. As if that were any concern of mine. Or in order to reassure me, she'll tell me she's not expecting, and she's not with child. Actually, she's in her sixth month, just look at that cute little belly!, but I mustn't be concerned, she'll take the responsibility. Besides, it's sure to be a boy. *One hundred per cent.* And she slaps me on the back. She's got to have everything right away, as if life, her life, were a fast-forward film. I had hardly lain . . . I had hardly lain down by her side, and already she was agonizing over how to bring up her future progeny. Languages. Nothing beats languages. But don't you lose any sleep over it, I'll find a way. The Goethe Institute! Still, she's not inconsiderate. When she sees it weighing on me, relax, she says, you're not the only man in the world (in order to soothe my sense of responsibility, no doubt). While I, if I was upset before this or not, well, now I'm *really* calm, as you can well imagine. By the time I figure out why this rush, why she's rushing everything along like this, and why she's pushing me, too — vegetarianism and the like — it'll be too late.

There's this woman. She hates me. She kicks me out all the time. Dumps me. It's some sort of mania with her. She discards me, like a squeezed lemon. She goes about it intelligently, though, with impeccable logic, and with recourse to a number of reasons why it should end. Why it is time to end it. We're both busy, she's busy and I'm busy, consequently, we get around to this discussion, this act, mostly in bed. I – how shall I put it? – wilt under the weight of her argument. Still, I didn't think it was such a catastrophe that our bodies were not burning with fire. A bit of fiddling too has been known to work miracles. Besides, I like lying by her side, my hand resting in her lap. That's not what she's talking about, she's talking about the whole thing, I get hung up on details, and details, by their very nature, are always partially all right. But the whole thing is *not* all right. We're ridiculous. A sorry lot. That's how she likes to begin. At which I push her thighs further up. Her slender thighs, I might add. It has lasted long enough, she says. Without further ado, I turn her towards me, what I mean is, her breasts. Couldn't we manage without these vague thoughts about the whole, and concentrate on flesh, bones and sinews? Well? Well, that's not what she's talking about. She's talking about the fact – and there's no getting around it – that there is something insubstantial about the whole thing, and that's far worse, even, than tedium, boredom, or a bad cliché.

I can't find myself in bed!

At which I kick her off myself, bust and all, and uncover my genitals, what I mean is, my prick, hey-ho, tally-ho! here I am!

She doesn't say anything. If you leave me, I'll kill you, I say, and force her head into the pillow. A good sentence, that, she whines, it does the trick every time, but even if you killed me, it'd be like you were just imagining it. You might be offended at what I am about to say, I say, but can you forgive me? There is nothing, she says, to forgive.

she loves me...**17**

There's this woman. She loves me. I told her she could kick me out. You scared the shit out of me, she later said. I was thinking the worst. But I never did find out what that worst might be. She could release me, let me go, give me up, put out my hide. I offered to go, and good riddance to me. My reasons were physical in nature. My body was covered with some sort of foul rash, first around the 'wings', the bones of the shoulder blades, with me flapping wildly and writhing, then I noticed the rash climbing up the back of my hand, creeping under my shirtsleeves, like soldiers, like ants. Next it was my lower arm. Then below the rump bone. Then the neck. Turning round and round with two mirrors, I tried to assess the full extent of the damage. There is something disgusting about me, I finally said. She nodded. She watched ecstatically as the rashes burst open or developed into minuscule boils with yellow centres that let off a sulphurous, decaying stench. She was crazy about them, she fondled and kissed them, she smeared herself with their juices. It was horrible. I counted for nothing, only my boils. And so the summer passed. By autumn the wounds and abscesses had dried up, the rashes, pimples and blisters had all shrivelled to nothing. She doesn't give a hoot about me, it's my body she worships, she sits beside it or goes trailing after it; in short, she won't leave my side, hoping they will reappear.

There's this woman. She hates me. Right now she is reading *Mein Körper, das Ferkel*, by Reinhard P. Gruber. My body, the pig, she says. My body, the sow. Momentarily, she said, I am in India with my body. I came along only because I didn't want her to fend for herself. She's been through so much in the recent past. In December, I even fractured her breastbone. She didn't take it too well. I had to go and lie in with her at the emergency ward. I can't complain about the care, but she, my body, was constantly paining me. Stop it! I said to her in no uncertain terms. But she just laughed and went on hurting. I didn't do it on purpose, I insisted. But she just went on hurting. Hurting me. Have it your way, I said, I'll take you to India, to Goa. You'll feel better there. That's where the hippies are. There, everybody feels like a million dollars.

So now, here we are. I take her out every day. She can be her naked self. She's gonna get a great tan on the sly. Before breakfast, we go for a swim, then we make tea and

43

toast. That's our breakfast. At noon we splash a bit of coconut oil on top of the tan. We wouldn't want people saying we came to India for nothing. We switch on the ceiling fan. My body sweats and shivers, sweats and shivers. I get a bottle of beer, she gets the fan.

And now, she's sick again. Had I known, I wouldn't have come. Her nose is running. It's been running for four days and four nights, I swear, though it's the one thing that was running the least of all. Everything *but* that. What have I done to deserve this? Outside the brilliant Indian sunshine, inside, this snot factory. I wish to God she'd sweat herself half to death, seeing how she won't let me go outside. She has it coming. Back home she used to try her luck with gout, but that won't work here, it's too hot, there's not enough pork, and certainly not enough booze. Around here even the sickliest body would be hard put to produce a proper case of gout. Four days, and the runny nose, it better be gone. Pigs with wet snouts we are not. No more running juices.

My body is a sow. She'll take whatever she gets. Fenny, that's a type of brandy, she won't even balk at that. Fish, rice, eggs, vegetables, bananas, coconuts, mango – I place it in front of her, and she shovels it in. Beer, tea, brandy, lemonade, milk, and down the gullet it goes. Instead of an answer, the pig just grunts. I've arranged a sunburn for her. She had it coming. Two motionless hours under the noonday sun, on the beach, in the sand. Just so there's no mistaking who's the boss around here. I can whistle a different tune, I can bare my teeth. Just wait till we get home! (I have the ticket, while she won't get any more money out of me. So she's got to come along.) If she thinks she can fool around with me, she's got another thing coming. It's gonna be yoga exercises, not beef stew. A three-day-long hub-tour, not another nightspot. A StairMaster, not a double burger. A bicycle in lieu of television. A sauna in lieu of sex. Upper Styria, not Tuscany.

She's in her thirty-eighth year, my body, but she acts as if she were twenty-two, the hussy. Adieu, Goa, this winter hurts. Back home I'm gonna enrol her in a senior citizens' club. See if that won't break her of this twenty-two habit! And if she acts up, it's off to night-school! The Early Renaissance. For beginners. And if she still thinks she's the one that's licked the pyramids into shape, we'll go through Immanuel Kant, word by word, with special regard to the categorical imperative. We'll see. She's on her high horse now, but she who laughs last laughs longest. Back home, piggy-wiggy. Who knows. Maybe we should start a macrobiotic diet. Or I'll make a Jehovah's Witness of you if it's the last thing I do, and see if there's gonna be any more blood-giving! I've got an idea or two up my sleeve. Just don't come with the belly. Not the belly! The tongue, yes, you can stick it out, just leave the belly be, piggy-wiggy! I said it to her a thousand times if I said it once, anything, just not the belly. It's bad manners. Obscene. Shameless.

What? A beer? No way! This Caju-Fenny? Don't waste your breath . . . Oh, just a drop? I know you, fake face, that's how it always starts. Oh. It's for the nose? To cure it . . . Fine. But woe unto you if I don't see results! Fine. One beer, one Fenny, and in a week, off we go. Just wait. It's gonna be a whole new ball game, piggy-wiggy, once we're home . . .

Gruber . . . , the woman now says. What do you mean Gruber, and why? We're disconnected. Is she really in India, I wonder? And could Gruber be her new body? She's full of surprises. Instead of the sow, Gruber? What's gonna be the new ball game, I wonder? OK. So Gruber it is.

There's this woman. She loves me. She'd love me to be lean, scrawny, not to mention ungainly, white-skinned and red-haired, in which case, with the unmistakable, grating tones of stifled passion, she'd address me thus: I love you so much, I could eat you up! Not to mention: I'm crazy about your puny little body. Your purple hair, I shall put it in my prayers. And yet, she's not notorious for praying, mind you. It's more like metaphysical fault-finding. She is especially preoccupied with the Creation of the World, its why and wherefore. What could have been missing from divine existence that God should have decided to muck it up with the Creation? Because, admit it, it's mucking things up! Purple. Possibly, purple was missing. But mum's the word. She's got an antique countenance and looks at me from ancient, antique times. She's Greek, it's the Greeks I see in her, in the darkness, the strength, the harmony. Her eyes like a statue's, Juno's or what have you. Two fist-sized gemstones. Which rubs her the wrong way.

Gemstones? And she rolls them round and round so you think they'll pop out of their sockets. Her self-confidence is in the pits and she doesn't know what to make of my infatuation. A log with a circumference of nineteen centimetres is twenty when you sell, and eighteen when you buy. If a good buyer happens upon a good seller, they agree on something *in the vicinity* of nineteen. That's what we call business ethics. Her dearly beloved father was supposed to have explained this to her, immediately after the war. Lean? Clumsy?

she loves me...**20**

There's this woman. She hates me. She's as small as a dwarf, a largish dwarf. There is something antique about her, *smallish* antique, as if she had lived seventy or eighty years ago. An antiquated beauty. But she's got what is generally referred to as sex appeal. When she looks at me, I blush to the roots of my hair. When I look at her, she blushes to the roots of her hair, etcetera, etcetera, etcetera.

she loves me... **21**

There's this woman. She loves me. She has freckles and gout. Her face is sprinkled chock-full of freckles, the 'blessed, golden dew of Orion'. When she was young, they called her Red-face and Firefly. But when she passed her seventeenth year the tables were suddenly turned, and she bewitched one and all with her freckles – so many mysterious, coded messages. I think she hates me. I think I can't give her what she wants. In the beginning, *our* beginning, I charged, I attacked, I laboured, I sallied forth flourishing my sabre, but – *oh, valiant soldiers, what could be amiss?!* – she just shook her head cheerfully. The cheerfulness scared me, my helplessness did not. I made up my mind to relax, I slowed down, I became indulgent, I watched our bodies to see what they wanted, then obediently did their bidding. This, I think, worked. At any rate, I enjoyed myself, and was inordinately surprised that she did not, or, at least, not nearly as much. On the one hand, the cheerfulness was gone, which comforted me. On the other hand, I counted her freckles several times, but never got the same number twice. I can't be counted, she said impertinently.

Apart from the gout, I wish to mention two other circumstances. The other day she said, as if in passing, without critical intent, gently, and – that's why I remembered it – sadly, or so it seemed to me, that she seemed to have detected an aura of dignity about me of late. And so, when in response to my more cheerful than boastful comment that today, that day, I had had a good day, she said that it was obvious from the tone of my voice, I asked if that was supposed to be another criticism, to which she said no, oh, I wouldn't *dare*. This puzzled me. We're talking, really, about *her* lack of confidence, she said. She had a long chat the other day with her girlfriend about the so-called mystery of Life with a capital L, and it made her sad. Melancholy. By the way, she thinks, she's been told, that sadness is personal, while melancholy is general in nature. I shrugged it off. Is that why you're sad? I was taken aback by her answer, which was brief and to the point: of course not, it's you. I broke out in a sweat. Fool that I am, at first I was even proud. Another time she said, remember this, remember it once and for all – and here she glanced at me and I, elated, promptly remembered everything – but then she went on: in short, you should take long constitutionals, have plenty to eat, and think of your body.

As for her gout, it was not typical in so far as the uric acid level, which under normal circumstances is a reliable indicator of this illness, was not especially high. And so, when the first pains came, the mysterious pains in the left ankle, and after the determination of the uric acid level, the possibility of gout was ruled out and medical gobblede-gook took its turn instead about the unfortunate coincidence of pulled tendons and sclerosis, which could be seen by eye, the doctor's, that is. Luckily for her, her knee swelled up, just like that, in a restaurant. She asked me to reach under the table and satisfy myself that her knee, down below, in the dark and in secret, was in the process of swelling. I satisfied myself. And when two days later it had to be drained, it turned out that the drainage, the fluid, was chock-full of those nasty uric acid crystals.

When we part, she makes the sign of the cross on my forehead, just like my grandmother.

she loves me... **22**

There's this woman. She feels about me the way I feel about her. She loves me. She hates me. When she hates me, I love her. When she loves me, I hate her. All other eventualities are inconceivable.

There's this woman. I hate her, or whatever. She hates me. She calls me April. A couple of years ago she talked me into becoming what she called 'vegetarians', which, to tell you the truth, I thoroughly misconstrued, because she was thinking how much better off we'd be without 'the pitiful wailing and whining of our bodies'; what's the use of puttering about each other's genitals as if it were mandatory or something, as if we were acting under duress, infliction and imposition, it may surprise me, her saying this now of all times, in bed, she said, she's surprised too, taken by surprise, that now, now, NOW! no, don't stop, that's not why she's mentioning it, on the contrary, though mention it she will, because it's now, when her body is just about to scale certain heights — and she is not about to make any disparaging remarks about it being a mere slope instead of a sharp peak, or what have you — it's now that she's thought of it, nor could she have thought of it at any other time, to wit, what would happen if she had to stop

53

now, and she came to the conclusion that nothing would happen, nothing whatsoever, what she means is, that she'd survive, that if now, now, now! when we are grinding away inside and on top of one another with such promise, we had to stop, it wouldn't kill her, whereas she should be feeling that it *would*, after all, why else is what is happening happening, if not because it can't happen any other way, but as things stand, what is happening is happening fortuitously, it's ridiculous, pitiful, or rather, it's like an animated film, it lacks dimension, as if we were merely imagining everything that's happening, in short, that now, now, *now*, our hearts are no longer beating as one. Hearing the word heart, my wand, as if by magic (or under the weight of her persuasive arguments?) – my prick, o Prospero! – went limp, out of sorts, I pulled it out and placed its hot, purple and supine hulk in the palm of my hand; so then, the woman then said, and truth to tell, she did survive it, what do you say to being vegetarians, while I, also still among the living, heartily concurred, because I'd been thinking for some time of trying it out anyway, seeing what it's like to go without meat, though they say all sorts of things, this and that, some have broken out in a rash, others have had their skin turn grey, their inner balance having been upset, while others report a new lightness of being, a cleanness and brightness, or bureaucratically, the need to purge the body of toxins that have accumulated there through the years, of youth regained. I dragged all sorts of books to bed with me, both cookery books and restaurant guides. And while, for the good of the cause, there I was, leafing through them, presenting her with choices, our choices, a brave new world which is just now unfolding, now, now, *now*, discovering its riches, I caught her looking at me, staring at me like a hussy, fixating on my dick, which acknowledged this with a blush. I felt like Little Tommy Tucker singing for his supper. This happened fifteen years ago. But possibly nine. And ever since, it's happened all sorts of ways. A period of transition, she laughs, if we were to be completely honest about it, it's a period of transition, April. And she pulls me down on the bed.

There's this woman. She loves me, though it might be a whole lot better if she hated me, too. It would make for a stronger bond. It would be just too awful if one enchanted evening she were to kick me out. Show me the door. And so I must chain her to me, no matter how, as long as the chain is good and strong. I humiliate her, if I must. Or she me. (*'You are my destiny, you are what you are to me.'*) Which is better? I ask. She doesn't give me a straightforward answer. At least we share a lottery ticket.

To make a long story short, she probably loves me, and hates me, too, into the bargain. But the question is, is she sick and tired of me? Up to here? Fed up? If not – if she loves me, or loves me not, if she hates me, or hates me not – then it's OK, then things can go on as before, I can slip between the covers with her, burrow my head between her thighs, go and sit in the kitchen with her, drink wine and watch TV together (on Sunday afternoon, it's *Zorro*), I can read to her (Karinthy humoresques,[8] and lately, from Ibsen's *Wild Duck*), and though I absolutely refuse to go for walks, I do help raise the children, a man's authority in the house, what money I make I give to her. On the other hand, if it's yes, if she's sick of me, up to here and fed up, then I must go into action right away. Money and payola, constraint and imposition: me on top of her. ('If a light breeze would help me get on top of her, a hurricane couldn't tear me away.') The abasement and self-abasement we have already mentioned. Anything, just so she stays. I can't just sit with hands in lap, even if the hand is mine, and the lap hers. I find no peace except in her. (On the other hand, after all the subterfuge, she has ceased to be, and I have ceased to be, there is nothing but the staying. But then again, that's what I wanted, that she should stay, that there should be this staying.)

---

[8]First name Frigyes, 1887–1938. Humoresques need no explanation.

There's this woman. She loves me. She just doesn't know it yet. I must constantly enlighten her on the subject. When we're in the back seat of a cab, I put my arm around her and whisper sweet nothings in her ear. ('*Put your head on my shoulder.*') Going around the bends, I overemphasize the helplessness of my body. When we eat I look at her, then at the plate, then at her again. At times I turn her around by the shoulder, there!, there!, over there!, I'll say, for instance, but as far as I'm concerned, she should be thinking of nothing but her shoulder. I regularly buy her candy, especially chocolate cherry kisses. Or I peer at her over the heads of the crowd, meaning, from the other end of the lecture hall. At other times I lower my eyelids. She's a dazzling beauty, a bit too dazzling, a romantic, mysterious Krúdy heroine.[9] ('The wings of her

---

[9]Novelist Gyula Krúdy (1878–1938) produced a novel literary technique hallmarked by stream of consciousness and evocative, leisurely

nose were as nubile as a trembling filly's ere she had met her rider.') Feathery wisps of hair lie against the skin of her thighs, veritably pointing the way inwards, that's how flat they lie. It is this wispy hair I am always looking for, which lies as close and flat and downward-pointing as blades of grass in a rushing river-bed, everywhere, in the light hairs of her cheeks, her wiry underarms, her thick brows, it's the only thing I care about. But my sole chance lies in melting away her fear. That is why I am habituating her to me, and me to her.

descriptions. He also showed blatant disregard for linearity in an age when the time factor was still crucial in narrative art.

There's this woman. She loves me. She loves me a lot. Sometimes she leaves me. From time to time, now and then, now and again, on and off, off and on, ever so often, often enough, more often than not, in jerks and snatches, fits and starts, per diem, per annum, passim. Disappears. Evaporates, like camphor. Like Kossuth in the fog. Is lost sight of, like Eeyore's tail in the woods. Melts into air, into thin air. The earth swallows her up. She absconds, decamps, dematerializes. Gives me the slip. Beats a quick retreat. Bows out. Packs up. Clears off. Makes herself scarce. Cuts and runs. Hoists anchor. Shows a clean pair of heels. Takes a French leave. (I should have it so good.)

She says nothing, offers no explanations, just goes and comes, goes and comes. It takes me a while to realize she's gone. That she is *gone*. For a time I assume (reasonably enough) that she's caught up with her usual chores, she's out shopping, she's at the movies, or it's her mother. But as soon as I find the first note, though, it's goodbye doubt, I don't go looking for more right away. I give myself time. I've got plenty of it. I turn it round and round, I look at it, I colour the sentences. I remember, and I fantasize. *I would like to see a world where people have more daring. The men. For instance, you, you never made love to me on your knees.* ('*A private audience in an empty room where the gentleman suddenly kneels before the lady and, adjusting her garters, he also talks about his feelings . . .*') *You don't show proper respect. But you make up for it, I'm not even thinking of you.* I'm not thinking of her either, I don't care where she is. *I've got to go around in men's overcoats!!!* The exclamation marks pierced through the sheet of paper. I am not jealous. Could this mean that I do not love enough. She likes hiding stuff among old, discarded dailies. No one's going to look there. Also in books and pillowcases, under shoulder pads, I've even found one inside the dishwasher, the bloated (!) trash can, the garden, under the mound of mowed grass, left in a bunch and well on its way to decomposition, the dog-house, my own shirt pocket. She trusts me, I feel she trusts me to find every one of her concealed, explosive love letters. And I do. Level-headed, or with a delayed fuse. A passionate spiritual fuse, a physical fuse. Outspoken and prudish. Vulgarity at a premium, anything to please a customer. Revenge. Treachery. Deceit. Kindness. Ingratiation. Honesty. Still, it surprised me when she asked, isn't it just like I hadn't even gone? You got on just fine with the letters, didn't you, my pet? That heart-rending search for the letters, isn't that so? The petty injustices that can't be countered on the spot. That stunned me. But I don't know what to do, I can't change anything. When she is gone a long time, I keep in training. I hide the love letters in the most unlikely places, then I have to find them on time. *Don't you worry, my pet.*

she loves me... **27**

There's this woman. She loves me. She loves me a lot. She's late. Constantly and persistently, she is overdue. And she makes me wait for her, too. She's had lunch with her father, she'll say, or she's been doing the cemetery with her mother, she'll say. This is how, through her, her father sends messages to her mother, and vice versa. My little carrier pigeon, her parents say. You should watch and learn, she adds, as if it were an afterthought. I wait for her. I sit and stare into space, trying to force time into equal slots, trying to count it, to corral it into the yoke of numbers. This way, even if it's a lot, at least it's not infinite. Or I stand by the window (in order to speed my view of her). Or in the meantime, I bring up her children, who, taking after their mother, are programmed for pleasure, while I offer them truth and justice. I am strict and permissive at one and the same time, scrupulously pedantic and generously liberal. A tight arse and an admirable grown-up. It's like I was their father – so there's not much consolation in that either. I mete out punishment in an arbitrary manner, and retract it in the same way. It warms the cockles of my heart to forgive them . . . I can ignore the fact that I am right (though naturally, I am always right). My paternal grandmother could mete out a three- or four-day punishment without threat, offence or spite. Today's parents can't fit punishment in time; they know how to threaten (the future), take offence (the past), and be spiteful (the present). Then we cordially review the triangle and the stag-beetle, and I ask them pointedly unpleasant questions about the topography and hydrography of Hungary. And nurse the older child's tonsillitis. When he's better, I take him to buy a pair of jeans. It's a circus. After a while, life returns to normal. One I usually take to lunch, with the other it's the cemetery.

I wait in earnest. Underneath everything I do, beneath each word and gesture, there stretches the boggy morass of waiting, lying low, like some wild animal. I feed it with daydreams, as if it were a vegetarian. I imagine the woman (who exists) having lunch with her father, her father grumbles because of the mind-boggling prices, though he never picks up the bill, he discourses on the blessings of home cooking ('Oh, those home-cooked meals!'), he remembers his wife's meals (last spring's pea soup with noodles and the stuffed leg of lamb), and reminds his daughter about it, too, who, as always, throws herself heart and soul into her food, she is a *serious* eater, deliberate, she looks for, and finds, ways of doing justice to the food on her plate, her relationship to everything that belongs to the realm of the senses is equally serious, and she acts the same way with me, bestowing on me the same respect and solemnity she'd show to a stuffed aubergine parmigiana. I count for a lot, I'm as important to her as new potatoes with parsley, or lox parfait. A shame I can't appreciate the lofty nature of my position. I imagine her walking around the cemetery with her mother, two women in the twilight sunset, no, that's no good, it's either twilight *or* sunset, they visit her mother's former boyfriends one by one, oh, how this one could waltz!, a lovable fool, he prided himself on his cards, and this one was *filthy rich!*, originally Steinreich, the name's German, were they all your lovers?, what an idea, she waves, only your father, poor man.

Almost imperceptibly, the daydreaming slips into worrying. Something has happened to her. A military convoy has crashed into her and I'm going to be stuck with the kids. Well, never mind. After all, I *could* sacrifice myself. I *will* sacrifice myself. I shall devote my life to sacrificing myself. Or would that be going over the top? I would become a bitter man, and the children would suffer the consequences. Fine. I won't give up a thing, but I'll take care of them just the same. (Boy, will I take care of them! As you see, tragedy has not blunted my sense of humour.) However, let's be practical. I'd clearly have to hire someone, a sort of housekeeper . . . Too messy. We're back to square one. If only the kids had been with her in the car. A head-on collision. Political scandal. The Interior Minister, trying to clear himself. I could go on wrestling a while longer with nothing. When I imagine this, worked out in detail, it turns out that it's the same wrestling match as now, a wrestling match with everything. That's when she usually shows up, but by then it's too late, time and time again.

she loves me...**28**

There's this woman. She loves me. She loves me a lot. She constantly gets herself hitched to somebody else. Then after the wedding, she cries on my shoulder, not to be consoled, oh, I'm such a slut! I cheerfully agree. Also, she invests non-stop. Secures loans for newlyweds, then flirtatiously suggests I do the same. Her feet are size 43, at least ('*Your feets too big!*'), and her toenails are chipped.

There's this woman. I love her. She's as gigantic as the Empire State Building. Mount Everest. The battleship *Potemkin*. A gorilla. If she should ever slap me, I'd go flying through the window. But then again, why should she? She's too busy talking on the phone, staying on top of things, sending faxes, setting up public liability companies, and what have you. She's even got some VAT deal up her sleeve. Her bed is the captain's bridge. It's from there she issues her orders. She doesn't wear panties. She makes her calls lying on her stomach. She pulls one thigh up under her belly, which makes her skirt hike up, at times allowing a glimpse of the dark shadow there. I call her Shadow. For instance, so you're here again, Shadow? I'll ask, hanging about? When I'm in high spirits, I shout playfully, it's the shadow that makes an old tree precious! And also, that as long as a person casts a shadow, he'll always have his share of misery. The sight puts wind in my sails. She presses the phone between her shoulder and her head, which frees her hands. An experienced businesswoman. Quick on the uptake. Blonde. And she loves me. Do you love me? she asks; of course, in the meantime, she's taking notes. What was I supposed to say? Well, old boy? Her use of words reminds me of a hooligan from the sixties. I want you, I say awkwardly. She looks at me as if I were the man (woman?) from Mars. My prick. It's hard, I explain. Rearing to go into action. Just look. While *you're* on the phone, and let's be frank about this, you're mostly always on the phone, *I* am busy wanting you. The plot registered OK? she snaps into the receiver. Meanwhile she waves a hand, what's keeping you, 'do your stuff'. And also, I also like talking with you. Go on. Go on. The two together should suffice, don't you think? Wanting plus talking, together and steadfastly, that's loving, no? She makes a gorilla-gentle motion with her hand, and as I go flying through the window, I can already see that I am going to land in the middle of a rush-hour gridlock, adding insult, so to speak, to injury. And I can hear, too, her talking someone into applying for a real cheap business loan.

she loves me... **30**

There's this woman. She loves me, I love her. She hates me, I hate her. She's been subjecting herself to various diets ever since I can remember, liquid diets and fruit diets, followed by the Hays diet, followed by the Jane Fonda workout. And now she's simply not eating. Nothing for breakfast, three boiled potatoes (no salt) for lunch, and in the evening, a big spritzer (white, dry). She's starving, and she suffers like a dog. On the one hand, she is losing weight. On the other hand, what for? It's like throwing pearls before swine, I say to her, you know me, ten or twenty pounds, I'd never even notice. And even if I did, it would leave me cold, I feel no sentimental attachment to those missing pounds. What could I do with the non-existence pounds? I'm no slave to quantity. And the truth is, I want the pounds you already have. This see-sawing back and forth leaves me cold. Believe me, I could die for every ounce of your living flesh. Oh, if only it were that simple, dear, for the time draws near when she will have a chance to wear that certain evening gown which for three years she hasn't been able to look at without shedding bitter tears, so humiliating did the difference between her wishes and reality appear, and it is going to please me, too, she swears, even though I'm not involved in the background activities, the efforts one might call technical in nature. I agree. An evening gown is an evening gown. But she's not showing results, she's not losing weight. When she realizes this, she has a change of heart, time after time she has a change of heart and she launches into high-spirited and excited campaigning. Let's eat together! And she starts cooking for all she's worth, brunch, two kinds of lunch (what on earth for?), dinner, two snacks, and a little something for unforeseen circumstances. She takes some to the neighbours, and they bring some to us. The Kárászes are good at stews (including cock testicles!), the Cziglers excel in cabbage soup. But nothing beats the goulash, 'our' goulash. These desperate flights of fancy between gowns and goulash is sometimes exciting, sometimes damn annoying. The truth is, we're fed up to here with each other.

There's this woman. She . . . uh . . . loves me.
She keeps pestering me with her goulash. Trying to butter
me up. I warned her to desist, refrain, cease, and stop this
thing, it reminds me of my mother; with the passage of
time, my mother's memory lives on mainly as an adjunct
of her goulash. 'Your mother's goulash.' What a sorry cliché.
And yet, that's the way the ball bounces.

Ever since, she's been tied up in knots. No matter what
I say, whether I am disarming, thoughtful, or lay bare (!)
my love for her, or am as rude as you please, I can't even
get to first base with her. Whatever I may do, whatever I
may have done, will have done, have had done, on the day
appointed for the meal – it's not dinner and it's not lunch,
but more like an afternoon snack and brunch combined,
in short, it would be best to call the whole day goulash,
not Monday or Friday, but goulash–, anyway, her voice
shaking, she pops the question, for years now, she's been
popping the question with her voice shaking, and, for

70

instance, she'll ask if *she* used to add cumin. There is always some question, some left over question. If I should happen to mention that we have already talked about this, she launches into an exasperated tirade, the gist of which is that these subjects, these problems, these matters, these difficulties, are interrelated, and though she can well imagine that I find it irksome, still, these interrelationships happen to include *her*, too, and how would I know how she is relating at this particular moment to the pot, because she *is* relating, and whenever she looks into the terrifying depths of this pot, into the boiling and bubbling chaos in the making, sorry, but that's the best way to describe it, it's always different – *you can't step into the same goulash twice!*, but I keep mum – the brownish-red colour of the paprika, the ingredients that ever so lightly stir of their own accord from time to time; the potatoes, the vegetables (not enough!), the meat, the colour on its own, and the consistency on its own, the meaty, colourless tremor, its shank, shank!, there are no obsolete questions, and no timely questions, there are only *questions*, or possibly not, but as far as she's concerned, we won't live to see the *not*, and it wouldn't be good anyway, it would be downright terrifying, in fact, if she could make this goulash without a word, no, not terrifying, more like disappointing, which is not to say that she enjoys or is amused by this asking of questions, her anxiety, her apprehension, her soul's turmoil, she does not regard her anxiety-ridden drive for and need of perfection as proof of her deep-seated feelings, whereas she could enjoy it or find it amusing only if she could regard it as such (goulash as proof of the pudding?), and we could have saved ourselves the trouble of this gruelling detour if only I had been willing at last to shed light on the cumin situation, its role, its weight, its status, in that pot of yesteryear.

The word mother is not mentioned, neither I, nor her. It's been diluted, it's been burnt to a crisp, that's how we avoid the subject. And what about the noodles? It adds to her troubles that sometimes I get egg noodles and flat noodles mixed up. Her voice falters, that's how distraught she gets. As if I didn't respect my mother's memory *sufficiently*. To hell with all this eating! She needles me until I also lose my cool. So before I take off I call, distraught, to ask if the soup has settled down, because I never assume that it may not be ready, but has it properly settled down, has it calmed down, because it's no use starting into a soup that's not calm, I'd rather . . . Stop that fussing!, and she slams the phone down on me.

The whole street, it smells of goulash, I say with pretended exasperation. I walk around the apartment, sniffing. My heart leaps for joy. In answer to the unequivocal and partly lewd nod of the head I make in the direction of the bed (body language), she says indignantly, now? when it's time for lunch? I persist in sniffing. There is the smell of goulash, my mother's smell, and hers, this nice, fresh smell.

she loves me... **32**

There's this woman. My mother. Is it all right? I have a mother. She hates me. To resort to a male-chauvinist-pig expression, you might say she's third class. She looks like she's from the GDR; she's decidedly vulgar-looking (make-up, shoes, teeth), but also titillating as a result, a person who (once) while sunbathing on her back slightly parted and raised her legs, which made the flesh fold, somehow, at the base of the thigh, it began to ripple, and these ripples brought to light a bit of hair, including pubic hair, a sampling of pubic hair. After the ripple had died down, everything stayed like it was, on open display.

For years I couldn't take my eyes from there. No. I could never, never take my eyes from there.

she loves me...**33**

There's this woman.
And let's forget this she-loves-me/she-hates-me stuff for
now. This third-class woman (to resort to a male-chauvinist-
pig expression), painfully GDR-looking and painfully
vulgar-looking (make-up, shoes, teeth), but also titillating
as a result, now, while sunbathing on her back, slightly parts
and raises her legs, which somehow makes the flesh at the
base of the thigh fold, it begins to ripple, and the ripples
bring to light a bit of hair, including pubic hair, a sampling
of pubic hair. The ripple having died down, everything
stayed like it was.

Every cunt is different, I said to myself, gritting my teeth,
burning up with passion and fury.

I have two mothers. They love me. One is a blonde, the other a brunette. The blonde is always preaching, bitching, screaming, sobbing, bullying – first and foremost – her husband, who is my father. She won't go with him to social functions or to quiet restaurants. She sits at home. She does not love my father, only his memory; my concrete, present-tense father she does not love, she loves only the personable, slender youth she remembers. The youth she remembers is not unrelated to my father, who is still personable and slender, nor are they completely identical. My mother, the blonde one, had a fertile soil from which to launch into her flights of fancy, and launch into them she did. This father of mine leaves her cold. She observes him with detachment; certainly, she is no help to him.

The brunette helps me with my homework. My parents want me to be a good student; I don't, because I am. For instance, I have to recite the National Anthem. *The fugitive,*

75

he did hide, towards him a sword in his cave did reach wide — this passage gave me no end of trouble. I short-circuited. My brunette mother threw up her arms. She gives up. At this, my father sat quietly by my side, the brunette on one side, he on the other, and he beat the lines into my head. When I'm not looking, they hold hands.

It's enough to break your heart, I said to myself.

I have two mothers. They love me non-stop. One wears a wig, the other's hair is done up in curls. The one done up in curls is no beauty either, yet she's attractive. And mischievous, or whatever. The one with the wig has gotten on in years, and her tummy has distended, as if she were perpetually with child. Her smell too has changed, it is sour now, like pickled onions. But then again, pickled onions are delicious. I go for them in a big way.

There's this woman. The one with the thing about goulash. She loves me. You mustn't think, I say to her with an idiotic smile, that I'm here only because of the goulash. She turns sour, she clouds over and falls on me, she hits, pounds and thrashes me where she can. You bastard!, you chicken shit!, you filthy rotten shit!, she shrieks. I don't get it. I sniff the air, it's delicious. I stare at her as if she were the man (woman?) from Mars, though she's as much a part of me as the vine is of the tree trunk. She creeps up on me, and puts me in my place. A climber, a bine. Bindweed. Poison ivy. I peel her off, gruffly, avoiding any show of kindness, that would only put wind in her sails. Enough is enough!, fuck it already!, I say with pretended vexation. Which calms her, in a flash she calms down, and, breathing heavily, she glares at me. Then sallies forth to the kitchen. I hear strange, incomprehensible sounds. In a couple of moments I follow. I saunter in. Soon it's time to eat a little something anyway, standing, leaning over the pot. What I see is too horrible for words. I see the absurdity, the ludicrous absurdity repugnant to the rational mind, of her standing by the open window, shaking the pot like one possessed, throwing what's left of the goulash out on the street. Now, she gasps smugly when she sees me, love me *now*, if you can. She's right. I don't.

There's this woman. She (among other things) loves me.
And promises to come all the time. And (among other
things) she does. But when she's not, we make plans for
the future. Do I want her to lose weight, she asks half
anxious, half teasing. By tomorrow? I ask, annoyed.
Whether it's today or tomorrow shouldn't worry me one
bit, not one teeny-weeny little bit, the question wasn't
whether it's today or tomorrow, the question was whether
she should lose a little weight for my sake, or whether she
should not lose a little weight for my sake, and I should
tell her honestly if I don't want her to come, or if I want
her to come only because of the kids. Or the ironing. Or
because my loving heart, that great big bottomless pit, lacks
a love-object for a change. She can tell by my voice that
I'm in love with her again, and that's why I want her. And
have I thought that one fine day she just might get fed up?
  She usually doesn't talk this much. Usually, she just
comes, and comes, and comes . . . She's fine just the way

she is, I say. She's just my size. But then I ask all the same, how many pounds did you have in mind? You know, there's the heart to consider . . . and the joints . . . and your blood pressure. Not to mention all that colossal weight you gotta drag around on those legs! What colossal weight, you cheap pimp!, she shrieks, did you say colossal?! Have you any idea who you're talking to? Well? Or have you really forgotten everything? Where is this colossal? Well?! I'm going to show you every single ounce separately tomorrow, and if you find one teeny bit that's colossal, may I never have another orgasm!

This sends us reeling with laughter, it splits out sides, because if there's one thing she has, it's orgasms. When she plunges into an orgasm, she can barely pull herself out of it. What depths!, she laughs merrily. I can't tell precisely, or at least by a hair, just when she takes the plunge, though I do have my suspicions. I'll wiggle my ears, silly . . . On the other hand, if she tells me she's about to plunge, right away I feel that she's about to plunge, her face changes, it pulsates, it flushes, it burns, it radiates, it's hot, with red blotches, her eyes are bright, and tired, too, with bags under them ('the bags of idyllic hours'), her whole being is suffused with ecstasy. But it shows on you, it's written all over you! She shrugs impertinently, olé! And that now, in that case, she can't go out on the street, it would cause a scandal, it would scandalize the town, not to mention that green-backed monster, envy. But as for me, I shouldn't be so full of myself, the fact that it's due to me, that's not written all over her . . . Why? Who else? At which, bursting at the seams with pride, she shrugs again, oh, it's such a long and stormy life! And grins.

She's coming again tomorrow. I am as full of doubt as I know how.

There's this woman. She hates me. *I hate this situation*, she keeps saying, like this, in her best English (!), but in fact, she is really thinking of me. She is constantly thinking of me, she is thinking of me twenty-four hours a day. Her belly, it's like a barrel, shiny and bulging. I love the way it looks. She says in all seriousness that she is John Lennon's younger sister, at which I laugh and do a dive between her legs. Head first. (She is my invention. I have imagined a magic place in the realm of fiction; a table lamp sheds light on that wet lair, Dr Caligari's pants; the wolfman peering through the window is dreaming of democracy; the woman gives him it; the wolfman joins Europe; filled with self-disgust, the woman cleanses herself; she looks like Marlene Dietrich, a blue angel; the imagination, ever on the run, goes off in search of another subject.) She knows everything there is to know about John Lennon, all the literature, too, and the words. *I am sitting on a cornflake*, she says, *I am the walrus*, she says. I don't believe a word she says. Yet time and time again, I can't wait for her to say she is John Lennon's younger sister.

There's this woman. I love her. She's as fat as an American, an American *proli* in Disneyland, only they can be this fat, like a house, like a hippopotamus. Dressed up, in sheets, in togas, she's highly attractive, because what can't be seen I deduce from what can, and what I see is her face, which is plump, no doubt, but far from fat, it doesn't strike you as fat, I'd call it copious, rather, even dramatic, and not in order to call ugliness by another name or to hint at my occasional (palpable) attraction for what is ugly; almost to the contrary, this so-called dramatic quality is an adjunct to her beauty, and it means that this beauty is alive, animated, unpredictable, unruly; she is bursting with energy like a sportswoman, one might say; meanwhile, the delicate curve of the brow endows the ancient terrain of her face with the countenance of a young girl, an adolescent tomboy; as for the hard line of the nose, it adds a classicism and timelessness of sorts. A ripe, graceful timelessness. In short, you can find anything here. The abundance is very real. Even her hair is fat, heavy, cascading, maddening, impossible to curb, to restrain. Any attempt at creating a style is condemned from the start. It is an uncheckable, free-spirited head of hair, failure as triumphant victory.

When I see her like this, dressed, in sheets or togas, I extend this abundance to her body, too, this burst of energy, this drama, this freedom, this lack of restraint. The carnival of the flesh! Besides, when you're young, you're beautiful! Or at least, highly attractive. Or at least, desirable. An eyeful. A pleasing handful. Oh, come off it! Still, she is on the best of terms with her body, she neither hates it, nor is proud of it, though she is not resigned either. She likes herself, she likes herself with a passion, but more to the point, reliably, reliably *much*, with no fuss, you might say naturally, as a matter of course, and this matter of factness, this natural liking for everything, this shapes her relationship to her body, too, her relationship, her body-relationship. Acceptance that is not resignation, pleasure that is not triumph.

This horrendous mass startles me, it shocks me, it paralyses me; for minutes on end I can't catch my breath; it feels as if I were dreaming, and waiting, desperately, to awake. By taking off her clothes herself, she redoubles my panic; she slips off her blouse with a quick, determined move of the hand, forcing me into the role of the observer, keeping me at bay, whereas if I could be nearer, I could close my eye and possess her with my five senses gradually, one encouraging the other. It would give us a chance. But that's not how it goes. I can't even study her breasts in safety; I have no time to indulge in their awesome proportions, because she unhooks her bra up front with a sharp snap, and as her breasts crumble, as her boobs regain the shape that their weight, gravitation, and the character and condition of the muscular tissue have determined for them, they promptly cease being independent, something that can be independently observed; they are neither big, nor ample, nor awesome (whereas if they were, that's what they'd be), but become one with that unspeakable dread, her body. In short, the breasts are, first and foremost, contiguous; a (two) mountain range(s) of flesh from which, drawing towards the back, stretches what, in light of what we shall later see, is a thin fold; but again, there is no time to reflect on this geometry (how these two connect to the presumable tighter plateau of the back, and from the two sides to each other, how the two bulging hulks of flesh get along, how they interface, deflate or swell), there is no time, only this haste, this surging tide of nakedness; for she is pulling down her skirt by now, no, not pulling, it falls of its own accord; she then slips out of that, too, like her blouse, freeing herself of them with ease, like one who is also on good terms with her clothes and is not afraid of them, but finds pleasure in them, if need be, casting them off, if need be, pulling them on.

What happens next is beyond one's wildest imaginings. Forget Fellini's towering women, forget the Great Mother, forget, in fact, women in general. Also men. Also mankind. And forget the colour white. Relegate it to oblivion. That white, that distasteful flesh-white will not bear comparison; everything must be relegated to oblivion; everything is itself; nothing is like anything else; oh, how terrifying, a world without similes, how threatening, how incalculable; it cannot be compared either to snow or alabaster or snow-flakes, porcelain, or edelweiss, it is not pale, or bloodless, or even deadly white, though incontrovertibly there is something lifeless about it, not inorganic, obviously, yet removed from life. It is across this unfamiliar, one of a kind, terrifying whiteness, colour and matter, that the new folds and rolls of flesh stretch, but especially pendants and dangles of flesh. The belly, for instance, is not a barrel or some sort of tub, but a bunch of enormous leaf-lard petals heaped on top of each other.

There's no getting used to it. And there's nothing redeeming about it either, not even its oddity. Or just barely, though to tell the truth, it doesn't put me off either. When she turns part way on her stomach, she's got to pee, it's pressing on my bladder, she says every time. Also, the sphincter muscles might have grown lax with time. It was the same way when I was twenty. You can't make love to her in ways that the world regards as more or less traditional, you can't unite with her like that, because these dangling, drooping, pendulous petals bar the way and obstruct my passage, forcing me into a detour. Her backside is not two (massive, etc.) half-orbs with a golden ridge separating them, but some *thing* of hills and dales, no sweet Pannonian or gentle Tuscan reminiscences here, but decrepit unfamiliarity and weightiness, dilapidated backyards, junk-yards, rusts and seepages, sludge, a garbage dump where you can't get your bearings. Ah! all that clumsy groping about, turning and twisting, all the false starts! And it's as if her body surprised her, too. Not that I was the first man in, in her life, but clearly, she must point a different way for each. I reach myself through my men, she whispers.

In the end, two routes, two major thoroughfares, were made available to me. But due to my deeply engrained sense of old-fashioned modesty, I'd rather not go into detail, though it is about these two routes I should be talking, if anything, for this woman is identical to these two routes, through which I pass up and down, in and out, the way Kafka's hero stands, his whole life, at the gates of the Law. This is my lot. There is nothing else. Anyone who has been given the chance to tread along these two routes – me! me! – can justly feel that as long as he can, he is the lord of life. Before and after, white leaf-lard.

There's this woman. She loves me. I don't know who she is. We haven't been introduced. She's sitting across from me in the restaurant. (If things should turn out as I hope, we'd come here a lot, and look down our noses at those couples who order the same thing; to look down our noses at ourselves, for that we wouldn't have the nerve. Asparagus season – this particular vertigo I won't even go into. We'd eat from each other's plate, we'd feed each other, and it wouldn't surprise me if this were to put others off.) You wouldn't believe the amount she eats, she gobbles it up, she shovels it in. Disgusting! She orders one dish after another. Her thighs quiver, her privates are as coarse as horsehair. I would like us to get acquainted. I think I'll call her Amalia. It'll bring me that much closer.

There's this woman. She loves me, I love her. She hates me, I hate her. You'd think she was my wife. Frightening, everything that can be described through a single simile is dangerous, frightening, unpredictable. And yet, everything about this woman is as if . . . as if she were as fragile as a bird. A feather. When I place my hand on her back, I can feel the palpitations of her heart. (She has light chicken breasts.) I feel her shoulder-blade, too, as if she had wings, stumps for wings. When it itches, I scratch it. Her bones are elegant, and then I haven't said the half of it. Her thinking bears a striking resemblance to that of Katinka Andrássy, Mihály Károlyi's wife,[10] in so far as she regards the world as a whole. Only global thoughts occupy

---

[10]Known as the Red Countess, the aristocratic Katinka Andrássy was at least as liberal as her husband, Mihály Károlyi, made Hungary's first president in January 1919. Though in office only for a few months, Károlyi initiated major land reforms.

her mind, general humanitarian obligations, civilizational problems, ozone layers, Kurdish militants, Afghans, Chechens, Rwanda, Romanian orphanages, Brazilian rainforests, Serbian concentration camps, Somalian hunger. Her hands are also feather-light. She touches me as if bugs (vermin, but never mind) were crawling up my arm. And so, when she's away – to take clothing to Transylvania, to organize a top-secret Serbo-Croatian meeting in Zagreb, to march (with four others) on behalf of the hippopotamus in Vienna – I walk around the garden, inspecting ant-hills, checking up on hornets' nests (the other day they settled in the letter box and I had to prod the post out with a stick); I get absorbed in following, at close range, the rather unequal struggles between the flies and the spiders; I am not even put off by the earwig (though as far as that goes, they do scare me); and when the time comes (it coincides with asparagus season), I review the troops among the May beetles. She approaches everything on a theoretical basis, me included, and even her own bones, though they are the most titillating bones in the world, the foundation-stones of the sensual universe. But don't go thinking we complement each other, the theoretical (her) and the concrete (me). While I'm busy copping a feel, she's busy puzzling over me in the light of my own relatedness. If I'm all pains, she's all brains. This sounds as if everything were in order, as if there existed a bridge between Heaven and Earth, let's say, whereas it's just language having a good laugh at our expense.

There's this woman. She loves me. But it's not about to kill her. I was a personable, slender youth when once I took her snow flowers, though I don't usually take snow flowers to women (or gladioli), yet from time to time it happens that I take a woman snow flowers (more rarely gladioli). When this happens, I instantly, and always unexpectedly, feel pangs of conscience, the numbing, cloying feeling of treachery. When I told her about this she nodded vigorously, in approval of my self-disgust. With the same effort, she declared, and shoved the flowers in a vase, you could just as easily fall in love with me. And quickly, without further ado, she pulled up her skirt to reveal her thigh, the inner side of her thigh, the mangled black stocking. A horrible spectacle, a howling crater, like an explosion. You'd think a tiger had mauled it. You could almost see the parallel destruction of its lethal claws. The nylon threads and black pieces flapping on the surface of the unsightly white flesh. *I am about to engage the tiger in*

mortal combat. (Ever since, at the most unexpected times –
on the Ides of March, at football games, the screening of
the Bergman film, *The Seventh Seal*, or when she gets her
period, or when another portion of the new freeway is
inaugurated, or right after the aperitif, or when we burn
the litter, during the washing of dishes, the changing of
nappies, or when one of us catches the flu, or when the
pollen count is alarmingly high, when the hunting seasons
begins, or it's Boris Yeltsin's wedding anniversary, or on
Constitution Day, or when a knee wound turns septic, and
also at the time of Little Nell's death – I repeat, with the
necessary alterations in the conjugation, of course, with
the same effort, I could just as well fall in love with you.)

she loves me... **43**

There's this woman. She hates me. I love her. Her legs, they're so gorgeous, it makes my head reel. Spectacular. Or is it just her stockings? The taupe colour, the gleam of the silver spangles, the discretely old-fashioned garters? What're you gawking at? she turns arrogantly on me, you think it says there who I am? . . . I nod impertinently, yes, in a certain sense it does, then I look at a thigh – and therefore, by definition, a stocking, and I know . . . She snaps at me: What I'm all about?! I nod, yes, indeed. This was a long time ago (re: personable, slender). Since then, she has wrapped her legs around my neck God only knows how many millions of times, with me drilling my face into the silver-spangled gleam of her taupe-coloured thighs, but I still don't know what she is about. Nor do I give a damn.

There's this woman. She loves me. I hate her. At this point in time I feel especially devoted to her thighs (she's got gorgeous breasts). It is her thighs I love today, the inner, velvety side of her thighs. I could fondle and lick them for hours. She wears her heart on her sleeve. If she doesn't want me to stop, she says, don't stop. When she hates me, she says, I hate you. When she does the dishes, she says, I'm doing the dishes. But she also says, I will do the dishes. And when I or anybody else enters the room later, she'll also say, I've just done the dishes. (Leave me alone, I've just done the dishes.) It's as if she were suffusing everything with light, every damp, dark recess, with no hope of escape.

she loves me... **45**

There's this woman. She hates me. I hate her. But nothing is certain, because everything that has to do with her I promptly forget, except her face. I am devoted to her face. And she knows it. When she makes faces on the phone, because sometimes she makes faces on the phone, she'll say, I am making faces on the phone now. Why do you say that? I'll ask, and it is just possible, not that it has any significance, that in the meantime I am also making faces. So it shouldn't be wasted! she laughs triumphantly. It is from her face I read what has happened to me during the past hour, hour and a half. The more I read it, the more I know. If I want to know, I read it. If there is nothing there to be read, I don't know. I'm as haughty and proud as a young cock.

Her neck is covered with red blotches, her cheeks throb, paleness and a red flush alternating; what I mean is, first paleness alternates with paleness, and again paleness, which is almost whiteness, and it is from this that the red blotches appear, but no, they gradually surface, only to merge after a while, and then red flush alternates with red flush, and again a red flush, which is almost purple, and then it's into this that the paleness makes headway once again. That's the colour. As for the face, it is loosened up, ploughed under, turbulent and chaotic, traced over, radiant and dull, tired and resplendent. This is what my life looks like, with no hope of escape.

There's this woman. On even weeks (the second, fourth, sixth, etc.) she loves me. On odd weeks (the first, third, fifth, etc.) she hates me, but regardless of the week, she's bent on changing my life. One week, I couldn't say whether odd or even, she'll talk about our wedding, our fairy-tale wedding that 'everybody who is anybody' will attend, but then she'll call me severely by my full name, enough to turn my blood to ice. She smells of leather, like a new soccer ball. When I place it between her thighs, my hand turns blue from the cold. You'd think she was from Moscow, I say to myself. Moscow, Moscow, Moscow! Whereas a springtime cunt smells so delicious!

There's this woman. She lo . . .
She can't make up her mind, should she hate me? When I
see her come towards me in her light, flapping, beige-
coloured mantle, abracadabra!, I turn into a bore on the
spot. I could never manage to be quite this deadly dull on
my own. At a concert, for instance, I'll suddenly feel an
irresistible urge to sleep; I'll start yawning, my eyelids will
droop, my head falls forward. At which she smells a rat,
thinking it's *her* profound boredom that's affecting, pole-
axing me. And she goes and apologizes. Which instantly
revives me. When she's wearing a mini, though, it's plain
sailing. Her thighs (or her stockings?) are as long as a pin-
up girl's. Taking advantage of the misunderstanding, from
above downwards, riding a high horse, I can now converse
very well with her, I am kind, fascinating, slightly frivolous,
sensitive and lively of intellect. I can talk as if we were
already past it all, with that sort of ease and compassion,
for us both. It is at this juncture that I want her and when

she, too, could best answer the question, does she hate me or not?

There's this woman. She ha . . . When I see her, I have to take deep breaths. In the mornings, I grow faint, even. And fidgety. And when I'm fidgety, I can't stop yawning. Which is infectious. There we stand, she with her serenity, wisdom, God-given sweetness, gentle movements, tact, timidity, purity, chastity and sagacious innocence, and me with who knows what; I am empty, only she is inside me, her serenity, her wisdom, her God-given sweetness, her gentle movements, her two mobile breasts, her baby-fine hairs, her tact, her timidity, her purity, her chastity, the stirring of her thighs, the surprising shapelessness of her ankles, her sagacious innocence; there we stand, yawning helplessly at each other.

There's this woman. She lo . . .
She's sexy all over. Everything about her is an erogenous
zone, and I mean everything, her big toe, the back of her
knee, her elbow, her wisdom teeth. Even what surrounds
her is a zone. When I enter the kitchen, she gets the hots.
I can't help it, she says, grinning like a little girl. Everything
that has to do with her body is good; apart from that, there
is nothing good about her. Life has given her a bum steer.
She's been living alone for the longest time. (And *what* a
time!) Her son is the apple of her eye. She gives him her
all. She's even started a hat business. She's a hard-as-steel
businesswoman, clever, resourceful, ruthless. Whatever she
touches turns to gold (myself excepted). The way she issues
orders, it gives me the creeps. The only time I'm not afraid
of her is when we're in bed. In bed she is like she is with
her son. She gives me her all. Otherwise, she treats me as
if I were a retailer. A wholesaler, or whatever, in her hat
business. She's after money, and she makes no bones about

101

it. It wouldn't be so bad if only I could get my bearings in business life, in which case, I could anticipate trouble; I wouldn't irritate her, and she wouldn't come down on me; I wouldn't be underfoot, and she wouldn't stamp me into the ground. However, since I am a perfect ass in matters of business, I have no choice, and must clear out of her apartment without my clothes. I pull my pants on hopping up and down on one leg, like in some third-rate comedy. Even on the metro, my shirt is still not buttoned all the way. I tie my shoelaces running down the stairs. My precious, I say to myself when this happens, though the neighbours are watching me with malicious glee. They wouldn't dare make any remarks, though, they're afraid of her, too. Besides, they haven't even got the chance to escape that I, limping on one foot, have, that sweet chance, yes, that.

There's this man.
He ha . . . No. He's really a woman. A slave to proper
grammar. Always chewing my ear about something. A
participial phrase at the beginning of a sentence must refer
to the grammatical subject. Being in a dilapidated condition, I was able to buy the house very cheap. Now, isn't
that ridiculous? And it's *may* I and not *can* I, unless I can't,
of course, and *weekly*, and not *by* the week, and *enthusiastic*,
and not *enthused*, and above all, ain't ain't grammar, even
though it seems hopeless, and don't ever but ever forget to
use the serial comma! No need licking clean the ass of
public opinion.

Let me tell you something, she says. Take these sentences,
for instance. They are here only because you exist. That is
why they can be said. They can be said only to you.

But . . . but what if the person to whom other sentences
belonged, like these belong to me, has died? In that case,
do they exist, or don't they? You see my problem, they're

inside my head, therefore, they are . . . , and in that case, they can never be said again. Not even to you.

What sort, what kind of sentences does she have in mind?

She had a very good friend. Her name was Borsika Hámori, and she died like Berlioz in *The Master and Margarita*. A tram-car cut off her head. She saw it roll away. And this Borsika Hámori chased skirt the way men usually do. And even then, not many of them. Borsika understood Krúdy,[11] namely, that his hero Sinbad is not only sentimental, a dreamer and a bewitching male, he is also empty and must fill himself up, he must, he must, he must. Sinbad is about this must, and not the bewitchment. (Oh!) She was a hard-as-steel businesswoman, whatever she touched turned to gold. This hurt her, and she was worried about her, worried that people would take advantage of her, and they did. They met again each day, early in the morning, there was a place on Rose Hill, their usual place, cosy, by then Borsika Hámori had grown very tired, but that's when her time came, they talked endlessly, she listened to it all, all the shitty stories, because only a small portion of Sinbad's stories are gold-inlaid, the tip of the iceberg, the rest is the cold, the trickling, the trembling, the flight. A lucky thing she was around. Oh, there was no end to their laughter over all those many men and women, because male or female, it made no difference to her.

I heard sentences then that only Borsika Hámori had heard before. I felt awkward. I wanted to leave. She let me glimpse something for which I was, how shall I put it, not worthy, not mature, not a customer, just not ready. At this point in time, I am simply not Borsika Hámori.

---

[11]Still the same Gyula Kúrdy as before, (She Loves Me . . . 25). Sinbad is perhaps his most enduring and certainly best-known character, and the protagonist of many books in which memory is the chief source of the narrative material.

Please don't go.

There's this woman. She lo . . .
She had . . . she has . . . she has an ex. An ex-husband.
When I think of him, which is not often, I assure you, I
think of him as *our* husband. When I ask her if her ex is
still in love with her, she gives an annoyed shrug and says,
poor Karsai, he's not at all a well man. Karsai, that's her
husband.

He can't find himself anybody, a woman, a partner,
though he's decidedly handsome, tall, presentable and
slender, with dark hair, like that talk-show host, you know
the one; OK, so he's put on some weight lately, but you
can't tell unless you've known him a long time, in his
continuity, so to speak. He's lost his self-confidence, and
also his peace of mind. He makes up for it by being vulgar
and obvious. He's an academic, an Italian scholar; he knows
everything there is to know about the Italians, the Italian
baroque. But he knows this everything the way others eat
or make love, read or play football, or go for a stroll. He

106

doesn't stop to catch his breath. And what he knows he knows to excess, he overabounds in it, he knows more than there is to know about it, in short, not just in which small hamlet of Piemonte you can find the Zrínyi letter which puts any evaluation of Pázmány in a new light, a not altogether authentic copy of which is in the library of Frakno,[12] but also that it's no use going except in the afternoon, but not before three, because then the reverend father is still taking his nap, and not after five, because by then he is into his books, and if we know what's good for us, we won't drink his white wine, which he will try to pass off on us with honeyed (Italian) words just to take our minds off the red, which is superb, but he is too mean to offer it to strangers. His knowledge is universal (at times it takes on a blatantly Catholic bouquet), precise (philological chatter) and amusing. Zrínyi, the entire seventeenth century, the priest from Piemonte, the taste of red wine and the moment when he is talking about it are as one in his mind, you can tell.

When I run into him these days, which is rarely enough, he talks differently. I couldn't tell you what's on his mind these days. Cunt, he says his mind is full of cunt, there is nothing else in it. That's how he talks, and not only in private, but in company, too; he enjoys using words such as the above-mentioned cunt or prick, fuck and yeast infection. He relishes saying them. However, since these days people are no longer scandalized, and shock, too, comes only when people are taken off guard, or are too tired or courteous, possibly in love, and there isn't another world,

---

[12]Mikló Zrínyi (1620–64): poet, military leader and politician who played a major role in the failed Rákóczy freedom wars of the seventeenth century. Péter Pázmány (1570–1637): writer, bishop of Esztergom, and main figure of the Hungarian Counter-Reformation. Whether the letter mentioned here existed or not will have to remain shrouded in mystery. Frakno, however, is real. It is in the Czech lands. It also figures in Esterházy's *The Book of Hrabal*.

another shore, from which to observe this one, from where hope could be reborn, from where resistance and opposition could be defined, and effrontery can be called by its proper name, there is no such thing, there can't be, and so everything is slightly off, ticklish, slimily unpleasant. He hasn't got a woman, I think superciliously, which isn't even true, he's got a woman, he's got women, he keeps changing them, he just married one of them, it's bound not to last, the way she's embarrassed by him, embarrassed by her husband – he was just describing, in graphic detail, the effect of a colleague's yeast infection on her underwear – though possibly even if she were proud of the fury and vehemence of her husband's description, the inventive detailing, he still wouldn't stand a chance.

With the woman, or should I say ex-wife, I talk more and more about this Karsai. He's got water on the lungs, that's the latest, it's how he's stringing women along now, I tell her, partly counting on their sympathy (the mother reflex), water on the lungs, that's serious stuff, and partly on their playfulness, the playfulness of a child, water on the lungs?, let's go before we miss the boat! That's how things stand with poor Karsai now, I tell her. For a while she says nothing. Then, I am leaving this house, she says softly, as if asking for the salt or something.

There's this woman. She ha . . . She's a busy lady. Works herself into the ground. Rushes out to the kitchen and turns on three appliances at the same time, the microwave, the stove, the dishwasher. She even makes toast. And faces, too, like in the silent movies. One after the other, the appliances signal, flash, burr, whistle. I happen to be one of them. The men are drinking sherry, an old, rare, Spanish brand. It fuddles them with its sweetness, its cloying sweetness. It makes their heads reel. In the other room, locked with a key, the baby is struggling with the serpent. His older sister watches quietly, her hand slowly stirring in her lap. Now the woman is warming the clams with rice, throwing in pieces of shrimp for good measure. She chooses the wine. She sets the table. They eat. The men compliment her on her cooking. Not too dry? the woman asks with pretended modesty. As a matter of fact . . . whispers one of the men into his plate. How many questions like this can you be asked? The men say nothing. The woman clears the table. Her husband gives her a hand. They bring in the cheese. It's delicious. The evening is at an end. Her head on the table, the woman is sobbing her heart out. The two men, one being me, the other, by definition, her husband, load the by now empty dishwasher. The serpent is still struggling with the baby. His sister has slipped into peaceful slumber, her lips as sweet as sherry. But by then I am no longer in the house, nor do I give it a second thought.

There's this woman. She lo—ha . . .
I don't want to talk to you, she shrieks. By which she
probably means she doesn't *even* want to talk to me. If our
story were more epic in nature, she'd say, she'd have said,
that she no longer wishes even to talk to me *at this stage of
the game.* Anyway, that's what she'd mean. That what's past
is past, it's over and done with. It is no more. And that
we've got what we've got, which is precious little. Not
even talking. Since then, I do all the talking (as if we were
doing the talking). I talk round the clock. While I'm
talking, at least she won't leave me. But as soon as I pause
for breath, she'd like to bolt for it, I can see. Consequently,
I have changed my method of breathing.

I am taking lessons from an ageing actress. She hardly
has any hair, it's very thin, up front it's gone, even, her
forehead having crept further up; her forehead has turned
spacious, like a man's. She talks either of her lovers, affect-
ingly and without inhibition, or the breathing method. Her

lack of inhibition surprised me, it speaks of true freedom, and so it has a modicum of modesty in it. She doesn't appear on stage any more, I don't feel like it, she says, I don't feel like showing myself off, Vanitatum vanitas, I say, moron, she says, I don't take it to heart, it's as if she'd run her fingers through my hair, moron, no, it's not because of the vanity that she won't go on stage, actually, she should call it the boards that mean the world, that's where she won't appear, it's not vanity, she happened to be a sexy woman when she was still a woman, though never beautiful, or a sexpot, or fascinating, it's the passion that showed, my dear, passion was written all over me, I was a sexy woman because I had sexy men, and that shows. Growing old didn't bother me, at fifty I had a good cry over my ass, that's all. On the other hand, I've grown tired, my dear, it's that simple, and I couldn't give a damn about my audience. If only I cared about the world, I'd care about the boards that mean the world. I don't give a shit about the stage. Listen! To hell with everybody! she said triumphantly. Me, too? I blink, like a child. I'm as intimate as if I knew her, whereas we share only these two hours per week, twice sixty minutes, she doesn't look at her watch, after a while she simply says, well, that's all for today. And that's always exactly sixty minutes. And she never has to cut a sentence short, or a train of thought; the hour is up of its own accord. That, too, is just a matter of the right breathing technique, I guess. You, too, my dear, I don't give shit about you either, but you mustn't take it to heart, it's not you, it's age. Age is wearing off. Wasting away. Fading out. Age is fading out of the world. There is no room, because there is no strength to make room. Or the will. It's not selfishness. I couldn't care a shit about myself either. This is the luxury which won't allow for the room. At first I enjoyed it, now I don't give a damn about this either, or that, I practically wallowed in it, I'm free of this too, now, and that . . . But that everything?! That there's nothing?! I knew there'd be trouble once my backside began to sag. It's on the tip of my tongue to ask, why don't you commit suicide? I think she knows I'm not asking, it's just that she couldn't give a damn about the possible answers either, or the actions.

I gab on and on to the woman with my improved breathing technique, about Europe, the ancient Magyars, Mary Magdalene, Miklós Szentkuthy, János Bólyai,[13] her belly, edible flowers, snails, myself, herself. I do not talk about the elderly actress. I talk mainly of her, I talk about the woman, not that this will curry favour with her or touch her heart to the quick or make her listen more intently, mesmerized; I expect nothing, I just like talking about her. Especially about her body. The similes come in droves. You're like a fin-de-siècle picture postcard. It's on those yellowed photographs one can see this sort of belly, this just-so soft, maddening, resilient pillow. In those days bodies seem to have had an innocence you can't find later on. Perhaps they were not as constrained as today, they just grew of their own accord, and so we project nature's innocence on to them. The waterfalls! Obesity is obesity, that's all there is to it, it's not *fat*. It's on these faded brownish pictures and you that I see . . . let's take an example: that amplitude of the backside which all the same is not − is, all the same, massive − not a rump and not a barrel ass, do you see what I mean . . . ? Because of its agility. The thighs, ditto. As if there were no muscles inside, and yet they're like marble. No muscles, no fat. Is it the flesh that's responsible? She gives me a look. What am I up to? But I'm not up to anything, except what she already knows, that I don't want her to leave me. I like looking at her body. I kiss it

<hr>

[13]Szentkuthy (1908–88) was a writer known for his use of free association and his volatile heroes who in the manner of Virginia Woolf's *Orlando* wander freely through the ages, changing their character or sex. Bólyai (1802–60) was one of the founders of non-Euclidean geometry.

here and there, or rather, I peck at it, at random, biting it again and again, her thighs, her shoulders, her wrists, her cute little belly. She's like a statue come to life. The body hair, too, how silky! Yesterday the actress told me my breathing method wasn't going to get any better. Will you throw me out, then? She didn't answer. I grinned idiotically, I was scared, she's leaving me, I thought, this is the first sign, women's solidarity. You will never grow old, I quickly added. Pause. Do you want me to say more stuff like that? I meant in the future, should I say stuff like that in the future? What for? Well, I wonder if she's going to fall for it or not. Is she going to laugh at me, or is it going to please her? I heard that women go for stuff like that. You heard right.

she loves me... **54**

There's this woman. She ha-lo . . . When I am near her, in the shadow of her armpits, the stumps of her eyebrows, the rose of her rectum, the tremor of her sinews (back of the knee, Achilles, neck, back of the hand), the crater of her navel, the pleasure ground of her backside, I feel I don't know anyone or anything, I am in an unfamiliar place. Except for her, I remember nothing. I glance at my watch to see the time, and by the time I look up, I forget. This makes my head reel, my eyes grow dazed, my right arm turns numb. My sense of space changes, too. Is it due to the need for caution, I don't know, but it's as if everybody were dragging themselves along. As if I were seeing staggering deadmen. (In short, I can't even decide if the staggering is fast or slow.) Only she is alive. I slow down, too. This irritates and oppresses her, what I mean is, the fact that, for instance, I fall behind all the time. She thinks I want to leave her. I shuffle along so slowly that, in fact, this gives me food for thought.

she loves me... **55**

There's this woman. She lo-lo . . .
The only place she's willing to see me is some old-fashioned
café ('the throne of solitude'). She's gained weight now, and
there's something the matter with her teeth, too, but I'd be
hard put to say just what. She snaps them together and
sibilates, something's the matter, she keeps saying. She
makes sure that our conversations are classical, with special
attention to the unity of time, place and action. When she
stops talking, I say, oh, your voice, you sound so strange!
Nobody helps me, everybody wants something from me,
I've lost my head, and when this happens, my voice drops
an octave. You have good ears. Yes, I say, nobody helps
you. We are both thinking of me, she with love, while I,
for the time being, stand uncommitted.

she loves me... **56**

There's this woman. She ha-ha . . . I think she's old, she thinks she's not, but we won't let that come between us. She goes around in polyester blouses and glaring colours. She colours her hair (it's the colour of straw). The strap of her bra is grubby. Her toenails are chipped. She's like a waitress. She's attractive, and she smells of sweat. And also coffee. She likes money and she likes the body, her own included. There are no exceptions, every one of her blouses is too tight, they tug at the shoulders and pull at the upper arms, and her nipples poke their way through the polyester, as it were. The whole world has its eyes glued, men, women, children, grown-ups, young and old, Catholics and Protestants, the rich and the poor, the strong and the weak, liberals, conservatives, believers and atheists, gays and heterosexuals, poets, prose writers, etcetera, etcetera, etcetera. I understood this immediately, this poking through, this exclusiveness and exclusivity, this helplessness and universal riding at anchor (along with my

117

special situation, of which more in a moment). It is this jutting through that moored her to life, and I told her so, or rather, I warned her with the best of intentions. She started laughing, screaming with laughter, as if she had received some grand compliment from me, especially the bit about life. But I wasn't complimenting her, I wanted to turn the situation round to my advantage. Squeeze what I could out of it, for Gods' sake! Except for me, and I bent into the laughter, nobody sees her outgrown roots, her tatty clothes, the shabby underwear, the fungus on her toenails, they see only that maddening little nipple, nobody else sees her as a down-at-heel waitress, attractive, smelling of sweat and coffee, nobody equates her with life.

She gives me a scathing look, is it gratitude you're after? You expect me to fall in love with you? Or what? And am I nothing but these two punctuation marks in the eyes of the world? Fine. And what the fuck are you? All the same, we get along just fine, the two punctuation marks and me, we have no bones to pick with each other.

she loves me... 57

There's this woman. She lo ... (loves me). When summer comes, she bursts into bloom. Like the early-morning May beetle in the merry month of May, her numbness melts away. She dons colourful skirts with a biting edge to them, she's not even averse to minis, which, however, don't go with her years, though truth to tell, her legs are spectacular, the light blouses like sails in the wind, everything about her flapping. She doesn't shave her armpits. She's a heavy smoker, and her fingers are stained yellow. For some unfathomable reason, from time to time she tries to kick the habit, and then she suffers, of which she is exceedingly proud. Then she breaks down and asks, would I blow some smoke her way. The way she lowers her lids and sucks it in, I should be jealous of this bluish swirl. She is often melancholy, which I, in my own vulgar, uncouth and healthy way, mistake for sadness, and try to cheer her up. But my mistake brings her out of her shell all the same. Like a magician, that's how she smiles at me.

And foolish and satisfied, I grin. On the other hand, the law of the conservation of energy must be at work here, too, *melancholia constans*, because after a while this cheering up gets to me, and while she emerges from, I invariably slip into, this other shell of our own making. She does not try to cheer me up. On the contrary. She bullies me. She says she wants to have a serious talk with me. She is good at talking with me seriously, she can make me believe that we're not talking about me but about this seriously; this way, I feel less ashamed – but no, I don't feel ashamed at all. When she's melancholy, and that's how she wants to have a serious talk with me, the situation is more delicate. For instance, she'll call me Mister. Even in bed. She'll say, you, Mister, are my country. A fixed point. I have found a haven in you. And instead of laughing at her, I bow my head and think about how much I love her. Love as a thought – preposterous! With the passage of years, her skin is turning darker and darker. Or blotched? More like shadows. Her body has become a terrain of shadows. She walks a cock on a leash, just like a little dog. She drags him along everywhere, to shops, restaurants, railway stations, the airport. Meanwhile, she coos at him. I don't like the cock. He's called Charles, *Sharl*, the French way.

There's this woman. She lo . . . (hates me). If when she comes out the door of a restaurant she immediately lights up, and pronto, I spring the question, Why?, or when she turns away from me, stretching, clammy from the morning, and without opening her eyes, her fingers grope for the cigarettes lying by the alarm clock, and she picks them up, and the matches, too, right off I ask, How many so far today? I try to appeal to her reason, I refer to medical science, the statistics on cancer, the graphic lung X-rays, on which the tar (possibly tar) that's settled in the lungs like black frost flowers is clearly visible. I call her attention to the importance of environmental protection. The glaciers, don't they mean anything to you? (Sometimes, I have the sneaking suspicion that she is suggesting, without so many words, that I should think of myself as a glacier. At other times, as nothing.) The glaciers are a condemned species. Poor orphaned glaciers, she laughs, and blows the smoke in my face. My comments, smart-assed expositions,

121

disagreeable inquiries, grimaces, continual, sarcastic attentions are not meant to pester her, and she knows it; she knows that I am merely heeding the call of reason, I am trying to help reason win the day, and though theoretically she sees my point — after all, she playfully nods into my mouth — from time to time she gets fed up all the same; regardless of its object, in the long run consistency is hard to bear. She goes off her head and makes a belittling, contemptuous gesture which unexpectedly pierces me in the heart. I feel humiliated, which I can't leave at that, after all, how could I have acted otherwise, and so I don't leave it at that, her slipping away from me, abandoning me with the words soldered to my lips, gasping, no you don't, old gal!, we rough-house it, I grip her wrist like a vice, I see the fear on her face, this makes me feel ashamed, she sees the shame on my face, this gets her gander up, which gets my courage up, things haven't come to that yet, not just yet, and I grip her wrist again, it hurts, she cries out. All of which is of precious little help to the glaciers.

There's this woman. She ha . . . (loves me). OK, so it's not love, but it's not hate either. More like curiosity. Besides, she's like a Malaysian woman, though I'm not about to go into particulars. The Hungarian male, some males, he's prone to see erotic fire burning in the eyes and cheeks of Malaysian women, but if there isn't, he's offended, fuck off, he says to her, and gives her behind a shove, what I mean is, he swipes her in the ass, what the fuck does that fucking chocolate want here? the Hungarian male says. The Hungarian woman, certain women, when she learns about this, breaks into tears, dear, she says, dearest darling, and throws her arms around the woman who looks like a Malaysian, why don't you pin up your hair, dear? you look *so* much like a gypsy this way, so easy to misconstrue, and she cries a little longer.

She's curious. Inquisitive. And also, she can't sit still, which is *really* easy to misconstrue. Even on what you might call the traditional seating arrangements of a café she'll sit with her legs crossed under her. Bending forward, she wraps her arms around her knees and starts moving them further apart, but all this, the knees, are on a level with her face. At least, that's how I *feel*. (It would be interesting to know where her knees really are, and what goes with them . . .) Her hobby, no, it's more, her constant subject of inquiry, her hobby-horse, is cultural interpenetration, which is only logical, seeing how she's constantly taken for a gypsy.

To be perfectly honest, I am disappointed myself, if I can't discover erotic fire in her eyes. But I never kick her. If there *is* fire, that certain gleaming sparkle between repulsion and ecstasy, I don't write that to my account. I wouldn't want to appear better than so-called reality either, though, because whenever I catch that sudden dazzling plunge in her cheeks and eyes, I up and have a hard-on (what I mean is, a discharge of semen). Which she promptly notices, regardless of time or place, whether it's a village or a metropolis, Hungary or Vienna, a dictatorship or a multi-party system. Whether she is annoyed or proud, and of herself or of me, would be difficult to say. She hands me a handkerchief, to wipe myself. At last count I had 237 handkerchiefs. I would like to go above 1,000. From time to time, I think, what would happen then, but never get anywhere. Two hundred and thirty-seven or 1,002, it's all the same in the long run, isn't it? But maybe that's the Hungarian in me, the 1,002, the so-called Hungarian male.

she loves me...**60**

There's this woman. She ha . . . (hates me). I love her. Now and then, now and again, I could kill her. Well, not kill, exactly, I don't know what that means. But punch her in the nose. Smack her in the noodle. Smash a fucking plate over her fucking head. Or the pressure cooker. Which might be lethal, of course. Or plunge the bread knife into her. Not for the sake of the killing, mind you, but for the doing, for the sake of the muscles. The muscles need training. It is far less risky if, screaming at the top of my voice, I pick up the table, which, on the one hand, is no cheap amusement, while, on the other, for days to come it would remind me of itself, which wouldn't be very expedient. Motive force is the expression of desperation in the face of helplessness. It is the sudden realization that the conflict, the misunderstanding, is not remediable in the sense – simply put – that there is nothing to be done. In short, she is also in motion by now, forced to show her hand, just *evening* the score, like me. And that for her, that mis- (from the understanding), it's just like the table is for me. It's the difference that's going to prove unbearable. That's why I've got to punch her in the nose, or unite with her in some other way.

There's this woman. X. (She loves me.) It's more lo . . . than ha . . . but especially than. We're scared stiff of each other; she's scared of me because she's scared of everybody, and I'm scared of her, the person I don't know. Naturally, I have my suspicions. Our story began with her breasts. We became acquainted in the middle of the Kádár era, and soon the four of us were fast friends. They are hardly bigger than mine when I flex them, though it's not because of this narcissistic motif that I have made friends. I won't even remember your shadow, much less you, when I'll still be on the best of terms with . . . One has a cut in it, a groove. She was afraid this would scare me off. There's a dent. The surface, it caves in. She had said as much. I said nothing. If I had started protesting, I would have felt the necessity to protest, and felt, too, the possibility of being scared off. On the other hand, not wanting to work in vain, I asked what the story was with her nipples, because I had known someone who was left out on the balcony as a baby, and her nipples froze and became insensitive. Well, mine didn't, she said, sulking. I'm kissing her up and down. They caught the tumour in time. Her laughter is the most enchanting thing about her. Like a proof of God. She grimaces contemptuously. She thinks me a bit difficult, childish, my feelings, as a rule, are childish, she keeps saying, my ideas, too, like the presents which I buy or make for her on the spur(m) of the moment. Even in bed. When she says this, there's a mischievous smile, as if she thought it was all right, after all. Still, I wouldn't mind if she'd say I was a man, at least once, but you are a man!, she'd say. Oh, well, never mind. Sometimes I talk to her breasts. One I'm on intimate terms with (Howya doin', you cute little intimate thing, you!), with the other I'm all *politesse* (How do you do, duchess).

There's this woman. X. (She hates me.)
She hides her face behind her glasses. She looks like a toad.
She's incredibly ugly. She can be incredibly ugly. Her lips
are hot. But sometimes they're chapped. She's smart. She
knows so much about the Etruscans. At times I feel a
stabbing pain in my shoulder. The heating repairman
says it's the stone wall giving off the cold. The woman
fidgets nervously. She opens her bag, closes it, runs over
to the bookcase, puts her hand on a book, is about to
take it, but then changes her mind. She is ashamed to
love me. ('*People will say we're in love.*') She's not used
to it any more, and she's running scared. Her glasses are
getting larger and larger, I could fit behind them, they're
so large. Her coffee is atrocious. She turns to the Etruscans
for help. A pity they're extinct. She embraces me, but her
embrace is constrained. I knock her glasses off. I pretend it
was an accident. I wait while she looks for them, on all
fours. I stay put. She's wearing trousers. I try to catch a

129

glimpse of the barely visible stretching of the cloth on her behind.

There's this woman, etcetera, etcetera, etcetera. She hates the whole world, and she'll do you a bad turn when she can. She won't relay messages, or she makes up false ones; she makes the children fall out, and my parents, her parents; the neighbours, first with each other, then everybody with everybody, then one by one, with us. Though she denies herself one of the most efficacious of weapons, pretence, her ingenuity knows no bounds. She is honest (to the core). She refuses to hide behind a mask. She is consistently obnoxious. She feels bad if she can't *be* bad. She'll put too much salt in the food on purpose; sneaks last month's bus pass into the children's wallets; takes the receiver off the hook and complains to the phone company about the party line; stretches a nylon wire across the bedroom, and when my mother trips over it, she palms it off on me; at night she sets the alarm ahead so we should all be late in the morning; she repeatedly denies having an orgasm, though at times the saliva runs down the corner of her lips; on the sly, she tampers with the figures on my tax return, then writes an anonymous letter to the internal revenue office. This perseverance, this insistence on totality, this unflagging readiness to do harm (to be harmful), the ambitious craving, at all times and in all ways, to hurt, to be hurtful, well, it's like a miracle of nature. Surely, others must feel about it as I do, for this passionate rapport with life, it commands respect. It is destructive to life, with one exception. From time to time she picks out one of my favourite books from my library, and then she'll glue the pages together one by one (what I mean is, two by two). And then, when I take out a Borges, to reread the essay entitled *Pierre Menard, Author of Don Quixote*, then, as I hold the book in front of me like an awkward piece of brick or a secret puzzle, an empty shield of stone, I cease to exist as a person, or rather, I would cease to be a person, if only she did not hate me quite so faithfully, then, as ever.

she loves me... **64**

There's this woman, etcetera, etcetera, etcetera. Champagne makes her sick. It turns her stomach. Usually, she even throws up. Lovingly, my own stomach turning, I hold her head. Some *material*, some chunky something, issues, or leaves, even through her nose. She insists on a good brand, or rather, quality, so that, for instance, she's partial to drinking the Hungarian blue label. Haughtily she tells me that when she looks at me, her hands turn cold as ice, and her knees begin to shake. But I mustn't consider this a declaration of love, not even praise; I have done precious little to deserve it, either as a male or as a human being. Not that she wishes to make a mountain out of a molehill. And a good thing, too, I nod approvingly, for in that case the mountain, it might come between us. I have never seen her in one piece. I have seen her eyebrows once, the pair of them, and the transition, too, between them, the gradual thinning out and the thickening, and on the same occasion I was also fortunate enough to meet her eyes, her glance, which is gentle yet self-assured, though typically, I can't recall the colour of her eyes, even though a number of years and decades have passed in their observation, they might be brown, brownish, sort of brownish, and I seem to recall a yellow spot, too, like a cat's. But I may be mistaken. On one occasion I saw her hands. Whether they were cold as ice or not I don't know, but they seemed pale. I was concentrating on her nails, I assumed she was biting them, though this could not be corroborated; she used to bite the skin around them, and she still does, the crimson of the nail-bed on her thumb and ring-finger seem to point to inflammation. I have not seen her knees, so I can't say anything about the shaking. I have seen one breast from the side, it wriggled and writhed and squirmed and jerked; a cheerful breast, that's how I would sum it up. Her teeth are a mystery, though, something's wrong with them, I wouldn't rule out the possibility that we are up against a case of dentures here, which, let's face it, calls for an explanation. I also saw her bum as she walked past, consequently from behind, gaining distance, fanny, rump, I don't know what to call it. Besides all this, I would also like to see her hair before I die, her ears (hygienic check-up), her neck (I've already seen it in passing, from the front, when she was nervously swallowing, and something moved there, it bopped, as if she had an Adam's apple), I would like to see her collar bone, the indentation above her collar-bone, and her ribs, her shoulder-blades like so many truncated wings, and the network of bones, from the top of her head to her tibiae, as they form a system; I would like to see her belly, the fresh flab, and generally, the network of flab as it forms a system, her navel, and generally, the network of holes as they form a system, the hair below her belly, and generally, the network of hairs as they form a system. This is all I want to see, I am saving my eyes for these. (She opens the champagne by pressing it between her thighs. It's like she had a penis. It's me that'll have to lick it clean again, one of us says, as the champagne bubbles over. Which – the champagne, and not this incidental joke – reminds me: needless to say, I would also like to see her cunt once, too, eye to eye.)

she loves me... **65**

There's this woman, etcetera, etcetera, etcetera, for longer than I can recall. We get on. I love her because basically I am/she is sentimental by nature, though probably not cowardly; still I can't help waxing sentimental at the thought of such an immensity of *shared* time. I'm not thinking of shared experience, though, I'm not sentimental, I'm not thinking of what is generally referred to as years spent in common; I am thinking of the fact that we will die soon. I am not sentimental on principle, I frown on all this recently fashionable sentimental bunk, this maudlin, mendacious, facile deconstructivism; it's just the way I am, it's in my nature, my constitution; I'm ironical and sentimental, these two things coexist in me side by side and simultaneously; they are simply *there*, but they are not there by design, in order to keep an eye on each other or hold each other in check.

Ever since the time she complained that nobody presses her against the wall any more in order to kiss her, that nobody holds her close any more – in short, when it comes right down to it, she was calling me to account for the passing of time (the immensity of time we were forced to share?), probably taking me to task for not making time stop dead in its tracks, because that's what great passion does, *time stands still, tra-la-la*, this being around the time I was repeatedly called in to the police, being given proper summonses to testify in the case of a certain Jenő Goda, and when I promptly said I don't know any Jenő Goda, they put me at my ease expertly, I might even say convincingly, they didn't exactly confide in me, but they did drop a hint that there's one hell of a mess here, the big brass, though they do whatever is humanly and *policely* possible, can't seem to manage the *matter* at hand, but seeing how I'm here anyway, could they please take down the particulars, and would I kindly make a statement, if only as a matter of form, about the Jenő Goda case, but when I kept insisting, wanting to know (if only as a matter of form) what the Goda case might be, they didn't take it too well, as if my narrow-mindedness had annoyed them, they became distant and surly, they let me go, they called me back, socialist democracy, there was always somebody else to receive me, even a woman once, time stood still, she was perhaps the surliest of them all, her red hair done up in a bun, and *ever since* I do nothing but kiss her, exclusively and repeatedly and nothing else, I do not say anything (to her), I do not feel anything (for her), I do not think anything (about her, or our shared past, not even her mouth, though through the years I have come to know it intimately, everything, the teeth, the minuscule changes of the teeth, the relationship of the teeth to each other . . . there were years when they seemed to be made of putty, then God only knows why, they became like cement again, the tongue, the muscles of the tongue, not to mention the flapping of the tongue, the ribbing of the palate, the cheeks from inside, the blood seeping from the gums, everything), I kiss her and press her against the wall, the wall of the study, the wall of the living room, the wall of the entrance way, the wall of the back room (it's for the grown-ups), the wall of the kitchen, the wall of the bathroom, the glass wall of the winter garden, the wall of the wooden-screw factory, the wall of the community centre, the elementary school wall, the high school wall, the college wall, the church wall, the chapel wall, the basilica wall, the wall of the former Party headquarters, the wall of the home for the aged, the wall of the newsstand, the wall of the Foreign Trade Bank, the plastic walls of the bus stop, the local train stop wall, the walls of bars, pubs, snack bars, restaurants, hotels, pensions, the walls of the *Zimmer frei* establishments, I push her up against fences, wooden fences, iron fences, wrought-iron fences, wire fences, hedgerows, hedges, both quickset and privet, picket fences, rush fences(?!), and trees, especially apple, pear and pine trees (spruce, Scotch, and Siberian, that makes three), and also poplars, a young walnut tree, hazel bushes, rose bushes, the medlar bush (though only when I stoop), the garden gate, the stable door, the shed, the main entrance (Scandinavian design), swing doors, sliding doors, revolving doors, elevator doors, attic doors, wine-cellar doors, car doors and cars (two-stroke, four-stroke), taxi cabs, buses, trolleys, tram-cars, the local train, the long-distance train, ships, boats, rafts, submarines, hydroplanes, aeroplanes, gliders, helicopters, amphibious vessels, bicycles, motorcycles, mopeds, water-bikes, water-skis, roller-skates and skateboards, electric wire poles, telephone poles, telephone booths, electric substations, sales counters, pub counters, recording decks, music stands, pulpits, bookshelves, warehouse shelves, portable harmoniums, gas boilers, gas masks, gas bombs, gas pipes, gas taps, gas lighters, gas stoves, burners and turbines, gas bills and gas lamps, certain Gascons, gas chambers, gas meters, electric meters, cuckoo clocks, alarm clocks, pendulum clocks, pocket watches, wrist-watches, digital watches, refrigerators, washing machines, dishwashers, toasters (Hungarian design), microwave ovens, television sets, the hi-fi (no CD player yet), I push her up against everything, the Parliament, my father, a line of poetry, the Austro-Hungarian frontier, and, previous to that, the Iron Curtain and the Berlin Wall, and now the Chinese, I shove her up against the PanAm building, Notre-Dame, the Stephanskirche, the Via Veneto, the Szántó Kovács statue[14] in Hódmezovásárhely, I knock her up against whatever I can, my neighbour, my younger sister, Kosztolányi's younger sister,[15] my father I've already mentioned, the postman separately, the telegram boy separately, the delivery boy, too, the gas-meter man, the electric-meter man, the water-meter man, the insurance agent, the messenger from my publisher, the embassy chauffeur (Mexico, Denmark, Great Britain, Italy, Norway, Holland, Austria), there's a woman who comes to do the ironing, against her, too, not to mention the iron, and I push her up against my pencil, my eraser, my pen, my stapler, pen rest, inkwell, paperweight, papers and pocket organizer, I squash her against books, contemporary Hungarian prose, living classical writers, anthologies, dictionaries, reference books, with special regard to the three volumes of the *Etymological Dictionary* (I'm expecting the supplement at any moment), my shoes, socks, jocks, jacket, necktie, eyeglasses, cigars, the soup, the meat, the vegetables, the fried potatoes, ham and eggs, the escaping steam, even up against the smells, and also the thought of a carefully prepared dinner

---

[14]First name József. Chief occupation: outstanding activist of the agrarian–socialist movements. Immortalized by a statue standing in the town of Hódmezovásárhely, once a thriving agricultural town, then, after forcible industrialization, just a town.

[15]Dezso Kosztolányi (1885–1936), poet, novelist and translator with a keen sense of humour, for whom writing was a way of life and the written word an obsession. Increasingly seen as a precursor of postmodern literature, Kosztolányi believed that to play with words was to play with destiny. His younger sister was his younger sister.

menu, a Ferrari, the Szántó Kovács statue one more time, a glacier, a swamp, a number of Mexican beers (Corona, Bohemia, Negra Modelo, Superior, Dos Equis, Victoria, Sol, Indio, Montejo, Negra León, Nochebuena, Carta Blanca, Pacífico, Chihuahua, Brisa, and Modela Especial, among others), a burst of laughter, a cornflake, a missing conductor's baton, Laci Nádai, Elzvieta Viterbo, a reindeer sandwich, a Hershey bar and, last but not least, everything, my words, the spaces between my words, my silences, she moans, gently, her lips part, a drop of saliva, thanks to the constant kissing our bodies changing, the accents shifting, our accents becoming different . . . and our cheeks tingle like the dickens.

There's this woman loves me. She's got cold feet. What I mean is, she's got cold feet *in bed*, this I can vouch for. I slip under the covers, and right away I'm in a tither, thinking, when will those nasty frog's legs come in contact with me? Further up, her knees are warmer, though, while her crotch is so platitudinously hot, I'd rather not even go into it (it scorches the turf, etc.). Her feet make both of us think about the frigidaire, and the frigidaire of cooking (first the deep freeze, *then* the cooking). I love her. Admittedly, I tend to eat less these days; I'll try everything, but just once. It'll go *stale* on me, she says, looking around the kitchen with pretend horror, you'll see, it'll go stale, and she rolls her eyes, like in the silent movies. As we slowly and gradually advance from the cold to the hot, as we forget about the cooking, the frigidaire, her feet, the room, the house, the street, Budapest and the nation, the continent (Europe) and the globe, while the universe is resolutely approaching in the phantom shape of something very like a stellar

141

explosion, she whispers contentedly in my ear, go stale on *me*.

she loves me... **67**

There's this woman hates me. You make me puke, she says, you never said that to me before, I say, I wanted to hurt you, she says, oh, is that all, I say, then it's all right, yes, theoretically you're right, she says, and silently begins to puke.

she loves me... 68

There's this woman loves me. She loves me. She can't stay put. It's no use my insisting, she says, I might as well face it, she's already got her make-up on, she's dressed, she's got to go. She'll be late. Is that so? Well, she might not be *late*, exactly, but she wouldn't *get there* in time. Is that so? Well, she might get there, but all the same, she's got to go now. I'm lying in bed, she's addressing me from the door. Just a couple of minutes, I say playfully, and expose myself. She might as well see, it's no joke. At other times, at least, she'll kid around, pretending she's sorry about this eventless turn of events, and I mustn't jump to any conclusions, there is nothing she'd like better than to take her place, that's her place, that's where she's at peace, her world's at peace only when she can revolve round 'that particular diamond axis of the world'. But not this time. She practically shrugs. Why don't you just spit on me while you're at it, fucker? Why are you going on like this? she says, resignation written all over her. I start begging, cajoling, I cover myself up. She places a hand on the blanket, and wants to go. I grab her wrist, I want to guide her, she resists, we struggle, I tighten my grip, she tries to wrest free, I won't let her, I pull her hand under the blanket. Brute force is intoxicating, it is the irrepressible yearning of the sedate observer for action. Or the eroticism of fear. The sensualism of defencelessness, etcetera. At other times, as she was nearing 'the pith and substance' of things, she'd become more and more authentic, passionate and relaxed, both at once, more and more giving, yet more and more free, while the mounting aggression, my aggression, would turn more and more gentle and tame, more and more effective, yes, it finally bore fruit. But not now. Fine, old gal, have it your way! But you're not going anywhere till then! I don't care, let them wait! Let the two little pricks (meaning our two daughters) wait! I look at her, she doesn't look at me, though I wouldn't say either that she's hiding behind her glasses, she just glares impassively at the wall; I see no anger in her face, or disappointment or sadness or bitterness, I see her as nothing, I tighten my grip on her wrist, moving it like a paralysed hand, the hand of a paralytic!; she let's me, abuse and self-abuse, two birds with one stone, and what a stone!; she let's me, I close my eyes, this is hard work, believe you me; I try something new, I loosen my grip, at which she quickly stops, it's practically mutiny, she's staring at the wall, don't you think you can get away with this! Of course, this way it takes time, we advance only by fits and starts. Still, when I come, it seems to touch a chord with her. We must really go now, she says, and they do. Touched to the quick, I wipe myself clean, my cock here, the blue skies up above.

she loves me... **69**

There's this woman loves me hates me. Actually, it makes no difference right now whether it's love or hate, that's not why I ask, it's the need to flee, the cheerlessness and listlessness of one who hopes for a change from the infinitesimal effort of asking itself, the word 'hopes', in fact, does not express by a long shot that state of duress and helplessness in which change is not only a wished-for need, but an insistent necessity, too, the brutal and smile-provoking expression of the fact that things can't go on like this, with one minute piled on top of the next like new dog shit on top of the old, with one hour riding on the back of the next like two jackals clasped in battle, and in the meanwhile, there is nothing besides this sameness, with one day, with one year following the next the way the latter would follow the former, anyway, that's when I had to ask *when*, which sounded like I was asking for a hand-out, and how!, provided the hand-out was delivered by hand, and she glanced sweetly at me, with barely a touch

146

of surprise, and what about you?, at which I was quick to respond, me? any time at all!, any time at all! Neither of us moved. Then she gently closed the door, oh, I heard from the outside (was her tone derogatory? terrified? resigned?), any time? that goes for me, too! The jackal lives off carrion. Or is that the hyena?

she loves me... **70**

There's this woman hates me loves me. Actually, this loves me hates me stuff, it's gone now. I could count on one hand, I swear, the number of times I've seen her, though in that case I'd be hard put to say just how many fingers there were on that one hand. I am standing next to her, as if we were at a bus stop, the roles have not been assigned, the city hums, drones and buzzes around us, and I say, as if to no one in particular, you wanna know something? I think I love you. She doesn't know what to make of it. What I mean is, sometimes she believes me, at other times, she starts to puke.

There's this woman hates me. Hates me.
I love her. She's falling apart. Decaying. Her hair is falling
out. In the morning, a small round ball, a small bird's nest,
lies curled up on the pillow. Her teeth, too, are falling out,
though, naturally, not as quickly as her hair. Her gums are
inflammed, there's aphtha on the roof of her mouth, a
proliferation of pus at the base of her teeth. Pus, you might
say, is her most prominent body part. Her palm seeps, too,
even though the skin is scaly and red, and so is her
underarm, there the small yellow arteries work their way
round the inflamed, red follicles, and her vagina has a thin
yellowish discharge, it stains the fabric of her skirt up front.
Her nails are also falling out. Her toenails are not so bad,
but when one or another of her fingernails turns black,
slowly, mournfully detaching itself, in its place lumpy chips
of keratin and small knots of clotted blood appear; that,
independent of the person, is disgusting and irritating. And
I tell her so. So what, she laughs, all human beings are

149

mortal, aren't they? In which case, I say, that's what disgusts and irritates me.

she loves me... **72**

There's this woman. She loves me.
I love her. Right now, I am sick of her body. She's turning
and twisting right here, next to me. I'd rather beat my
meat. No good. Too direct.

she loves me... **73**

There's this woman. She loves me. Do you love me? I ask. Now why should she? Because we agreed. Agreed to love you? Is that it? That's it. Today? Today, too, of course, always, at ten-thirty, and in January, at the turn of the century. All the time . . . Or, would she like a day off? Fine. Any particular day she has in mind? What do you say to . . . to Wednesday? Why Wednesday? Because today is Thursday. What generosity!

There's this woman. I love her. I can even tell you why. I could list those qualities, those good and bad and unclassifiable qualities, that led me to this loving. She speaks Greek. She's got freckles. Her forehead has a scar, a pale exclamation mark. She's radical, with a taste for the good life. Her hair is luxuriously cascading, her lips are sour, her heart is weak, her thighs are short (one of them, at any rate). When it's very hot, and I don't quite know how to put this, the skin gets chapped under her rump bone, at the spot where the two mounds begin, but the valley has not yet bent into it; at this spot her skin cracks and is also somewhat inflamed. She loves Italo Calvino and oatflakes. Her skin is the colour of bronze. She is vulgar and vestal, at one and the same time, with the self-same, daring gesture. I could count on one hand the number of times I've seen her, etcetera, etcetera, etcetera. The fact is, I love you. She doesn't know what to make of it.

she loves me... **75**

There's this woman. She hates me. She certainly doesn't love me, that's for sure. But mostly, she just plays basketball. She pushes me up against the wall, she pushes me up against the wall with her crotch, the wall of the study, the living-room wall, the hazelnut bush, the wine-cellar door, Notre-Dame. What can I do? I've been out of training for a long, long time. And though I tell her I'm a mature man, an army veteran, and she should come to her senses, she just shrugs. She practically slaps me around with her crotch. Bending her knee, she squats so we're the same height, then she lets go. She plays centre, and her average is extremely reliable. If they ever make it into the national league, I will have to think of something, this is clearly not enough.

There's this woman. She loves me. But mostly, she just dances ballet. There isn't an ounce of extra flesh on her. It comes with a price, though; her neck is wrinkled, though slightly, and not like a turkey's, or like on Maugham's photographs in his old age; there's no loose flesh, though when she speaks the tendons grow taut or a muscle trembles, like the singer Kati Kovács's at that talent contest of old. Which leaves the backside dilemma. *Arsch oder Gesicht*, as the saying goes, face or arse (face or farce, I feel like saying in jocular summation). After forty, a woman's got to choose. The problem has been settled; the face is in equilibrium, there are no cavities, no unexpected ridges of flesh, there are no sharp grooves in the skin around the lips, while the crow's feet around the eyes speak of sincerity, and not the inexorable passing of time. She can kick her legs up to shoulder height without so much as a warm-up. And she does it, too, in shops and restaurants, from time to time, without the slightest provocation. People

155

look. I stand proud against their glare. She can even do the splits, especially in May. To say she does ballet is not enough, though; she is a dancer from head to foot, every part of her, from the cartilage in her nose or her Achilles tendon, every part of her, at every moment of the day. Our life is one never-ending *pas de deux*, tulle skirt, lead points.

she loves me... **77**

There's this woman. She loves me. (I have decided you love me, I said to her once, a very long time ago, though I mention this only in passing.) She has it in for the commies. As much as she loves me, that's how much she hates the commies. More to the point, she loves me as much as she hates them. When her hatred subsides, her love cools, and when she is boiling over with hatred of them, she is burning with love for me. This is socially unjust, but when it comes down to it (to me), what do I care about justice? For instance, during the first freely elected gentlemen's government,[16] our relationship was nothing to write home about. Nothing irremediable happened, it's just that . . . in short, we limited our discussions

---

[16]A reference to the Hungarian Democratic Forum, (She Loves Me . . . 7), who won the first post-communist elections of 1989. Later they were seen by many as overly nationalistic, and wanting to bring back 'gentlemanly' and outdated pre-war values.

to the household chores and sending the children off to school, and she never broke into tears when she looked at me, she didn't flee, screaming, from me in her underwear, jumping over tables and chairs, she didn't open the bathroom door on me when I was inside.

Not so after the elections![17] Ah! So you're back, are you!, and those cute little starry eyes of hers flashed like the very devil. They lay sprawling over this country for forty years. And these assholes went and voted for them! I keep mum. I'd rather not say that these assholes are us, the country. *I* didn't vote for them, and don't you go saying it, even as a joke, and if you voted for them in secret, I'm going to kill you. What a sweetheart. I don't even try to calm her down, I wouldn't dream of it: memories of Tuscany. Why, they can't even speak the language properly, she screeches. Inside me, everything is stretched tight as a bow, that's how close I feel to her. They robbed us blind, and now they're playing Mr Clean! They crippled this nation, and now they're shooting their mouths off. I turn white, my hands tremble, I hear the beating of my heart. Trade union lobbyists!, and she squeezes my balls, but with so much feeling, passion and oomph, it would suffice to rebuild the nation.

---

[17]As a result of the 1994 elections, the Hungarian Democratic Forum and the reform-Communists changed places in Parliament.

158

she loves me... **78**

There's this woman. She loves me, she loves me not. At the moment of le petit mort, *nota bene*, in the throes of ecstasy, I shout into her face or neck or groin, I shout into her anything, into wherever I happen to find myself, you, you, you *ombudswoman*, you![18] – this is how the end comes. I scratch her tummy. Our democratic institutions are in good working order.

---

[18]The office of ombudsman, or government-appointed watchdog, to oversee the workings of democracy, was reinstated by the new post-Communist government elected to office in 1990.

she loves me... **79**

There's this woman. She hates me. Actually, two. Do you think we're pretty?, they ask, giggling. The yellow autumn sun is beating down on me, I am sitting on the steps of the church, like a beggar, or a priest, heeding the voice of the times. A papal legate. They shall have my answer soon. But first, some time must pass. A group of Japanese tourists flood the square, we send the kids off to their first day of school, the two women are in charge of the humanities, I represent the natural science line, in the old-fashioned café across the way one of the waiters falls out with the girl who makes the coffee, they shout, then shove each other around, the long shadow of the church tower falls on the square, we shudder and receive impressive promotions at the office, our relationship to the body changes, we turn sedate, but it soon turns out that this was self-deception, the noise won't let up, our backsides on the cold steps are cold, raising ourselves up from time to time, we rub them (physics!), there comes a time when our children's lives are more important than our own, we feel, which we later regret, and when the bluish-brown surge of eventide has flooded the world, I whisper into the girls' ears that alas, I had had onions for lunch, and though I have brushed my teeth, it was of little use, for as we well know, the smell issues not from the mouth but from the stomach. Slowly, leisurely, they open their handbags, Benetton green, they each extract an onion, and bite into it with a crunch, as if it were an apple, in perfect unison, like the Kessler sisters.[19]

---

[19]The Kessler sisters are to Germany what the Andrews sisters were once to the USA.

she loves me... **80**

There's this woman. She loves me (or hates me). She's very helpful. Unlike me. Which gives her a reason to live. (*You give me a reason to live.*) If she can't help, she gets the blues, and is even angry, a bit. I must find her ways of helping. Around the clock, day and night, I must get myself into trouble so she can be tolerable. When the washing machine is leaking, I have it made. When it is leaking, *plus* it is clogged up, that's even better. Or the telephone line gets washed out by the rain. I lose my keys. The doorjamb bends out of shape. I have it out with my mother. The waiter cheats me. Or the cabbie. My ankle is killing me. My neck. My lower back. Or the mustard seed runs out. The nettle tea. But she's happiest when there is no apparent reason for my problems. When everything is in order, the washing machine is churning away merrily, there's no static on the phone, it doesn't give you the wrong number, the line's not busy and it's not bugged and feels like they're whispering directly into my ear, the keys are lying securely in my pocket, the door, you'd think it was hydraulic, my relationship with my mother is so harmonious, it should be bottled and sold at the corner shop, the waiter refuses to take my money and says it is an honour to serve me, the cabbie is on time, like a gentleman of the old school, as for my ankle, I don't even know I have one, my neck and lower back are flexible, elegant and lean, there's enough mustard seed to drown an army, and I supply the entire neighbourhood with nettle tea — and yet, she can hardly contain herself. Her gratitude knows no bounds. The look she gives me makes me hot under the collar. At such times she helps with such determination, it makes her flush; what I mean is throbbing red spots appear on her neck and around her collar-bone. But she does her best, she truly does. She has just one condition, that she will not touch anything with her hands. She pulls on a pair of gloves. Nothing anywhere, just the fine, white gloves.

There's this woman. She hates me. But only because she hates everybody. She's no spring chicken, but then, neither am I. She likes to massage me with her foot. She can massage me all over, that's how inventive and determined she is. The back of my ear. My nape. Or she'll zero in on the parotid gland, not to mention my dick (rolling it between the soles of her feet, or grasping it with her toes, etc.). When she's in high spirits, or comes into cash unexpectedly, or else, not unexpectedly but a lot of it, she can even produce mumps. You should see how I swell up! In the meantime, she talks about old times.

The time she was arrested, a cop knocked on the door, he didn't bang, he knocked like a gentleman, then hand-cuffed her. The neighbours were all smiles, as if they hadn't seen the handcuffs. They stood around in front of the house for a while, setting off and not setting off, until finally the cop stopped a passing truck loaded with workmen, and they climbed up on the platform, and the men made room

164

for them. The men looked dead tired, they must have come from work, their heads were hanging, their arms were hanging, they paid attention to nothing, and this got her, this got to her, this nothing, not the lack of sympathy, but the nothing, that there is nothing, nothing but her, and she found this horrible, unbearable, this solitude, the fact that only these handcuffs should bind her to the world, and that consequently, the cop should be the world. Whose face she can't recall. It's fallen out of her. A young man, short, thin, bones like a bird, on the middle finger of the left hand, two warts, twin warts. He had trouble with his conjunctiva, and the tears never stopped coming, you'd think he was crying.

I found this repulsive. I kept staring at the men, one by one, trying to stir them out of their apathy, trying to bring their faces alive. Nothing. They were exhausted, and they lacked courage. Not wanting to get involved. Understandable. Except, I couldn't afford to be understanding. I was in trouble. I sprang to my feet on top of the speeding vehicle, tottering like a drunk, filthy cowards!, I screamed, filthy yellow cowards!, pulling and tugging at the cop on the end of the handcuffs, swinging him round like in a period-film classic: the incarcerated hero with his ball and chain. My screaming turned into harsh laughter, this chasm between myself and the terrified bunch of squatting men could bring nothing but laughter to my lips. The cop pulled me back into my place and, after a while, I sat there just like all the rest.

You gotta be careful with mumps, your balls get inflamed, they get swollen, they distend, or else one of them gets inflamed and passes it on to the other. Also, it's painful and could wreak havoc with one's potency, though it is not incapacitating, so to speak. They must be kept warm at all costs. This, too, she does with her feet! She wraps my balls round with her feet. She's got the patience of an angel, her patience can stretch on for weeks, that's how enduring it is, while I sit merrily on my eggs, nursing them like some ominous black eagle.

And then all of a sudden one of the men on the truck, he didn't say anything, not quite, because there were no words, but he let out a sound, short, stifled moans, and he was soon joined by more and more of the others in this droning, this dead singing. They were singing for me with their remaining strength, they wrapped me round with their singing, she said, while she rolled me and wrapped me round with the velvety soles of her feet.

There's this woman. She loves me? You'd think she just stepped out of the pages of *Vogue*. She's a passionate inaugurator of new libraries. She has a fire-engine-red suit that'll make your head spin. She generally inaugurates in that. The last fortresses of Hungarian culture, she says, and turns her head every which way. The small feather on her hat trembles. In a certain sense, she's got me in the palm of her hand. I wouldn't go so far as to say I'm at her mercy, or that she's got something over me. But I'm afraid of her. I'm afraid of her of my own free will. There are a number of others, too, afraid of her. Her pubic hair is red, light red, a stone-washed pink, in sharp contrast to the suit. From very close up, at follicle-distance, it's like a forest of larch trees (*Larix decidua*). Not far from where I live, there are mountains barely taller than hills, covered as far as the eye can see with larch trees. When I was a child we used to go hiking there regularly, partly with my class, and then we'd play hide and seek; to this day I can feel the thousands of minuscule pin-pricks from the tree bark; we liked to hide behind the trunks of larch trees, partly with the local chaplain, on Sunday, when he held Mass in the woods, in secret, the excursion thus turning into the corruption of the nation's youth, and so, to be on the safe side, boys were posted on the edge of the woods, who self-importantly stood guard over the quiet hillside which led down to gypsy row, and they often whistled for no apparent reason, alarming those inside, which in the chapel made of the trees was followed by scenes fit for a burlesque, a quick change of clothes, dismantling, disbanding, then back again at the sound of the next whistle, *gloria in excelsis Deo*. I never had the nerve to throw pine cones during Mass.

The scene of our first meeting, of our acquaintanceship, was also a library. She was not just inaugurating it, post-inaugurating, actually, since it had been open for several weeks by then. It has a limited but intelligent selection; you won't find Wittgenstein, but there's Musil; there's no Musil diary, but there is Tsvetayeva.[20]

---

[20]First name Marina Ivanovna (1892–1951). Russian poet who wrote romantic, frenetic verse. Not the first time she is mentioned in an Esterházy work of (*see The Book of Hrabal*).

There's this woman. She hates me. But only lately, because lately I've been experiencing financial difficulties. There must be something up with the Gee-Dee-Pee, plus the rice of milk (and honey). But she mustn't worry, I'll support her, but she better kiss the good life goodbye: Italian olive oil and sesame buns, it's gonna be a different ball game from now on. Different? How? Right now, it's the how we're working on. How a man is supposed to support a woman. With one lump sum for the entire month? An equitable, scrupulously predetermined sum arrived at by collective bargaining? But what if after one week I kick you in the ass? That's your problem. And yours. Fair enough. In which case, how about every day? Or every time we meet? But then every time it would be about the money. After we had rejected the idea of my supporting her in secret – an anonymous donor, the discrete deposition of banknotes on the dressing table, etc. – we have now decided that on the contrary, *she* is going to take the predetermined sum from a prearranged place (inside coat pocket, hat lining, etc.) in secret. Because of the secrecy, it won't come between us, while because of the taking, we won't have to pretend that nothing's happened. And can I take as much as I like? she says. As much as you like, I say at long last, and mean it.

There's this woman. She loves me. She'd love me, if only she loved anybody. They say she's egocentric and infantile. Long on brains, short on heart. And only her garden interests her, the dahlias, and all that jazz. Sorry about that. She's expecting now, and she's with child. Being with child doesn't suit her. Some women get rounded out, they radiate, you can see the *plenitude*, the – an exaggeration? – joy of creation, while on others it's the pain, the strain, the burden. She's in her sixth month, but she won't let me sleep with her, she denies me her body. Ridiculous, but what can I do? I burrow my head into her lap, the pubic hairs stirring, moving, make music, early Satie, oh, the history of music, the incessant listening! (Apart from this, I could also mention the Haydn hairs, *in concerto*: the last sonatas, and also Beethoven's Appassionata, Liszt's Saint Elizabeth's Legend, Mozart's Requiem, and last but not least the Hazy Osterwald sextet.)

There's this woman. Oh, how I love her! And yet, oh, how I love her. The way she made me realize that . . . Left to my own devices, to fend for myself, need I say, I'd think that God created man in His own image. I feel as passionate about Creation as a schoolgirl. Since I know her, though, I know that cold anxiety, that grey cruelty, which comes trickling from God knows where, it's just that my voice suddenly falters, and I am shaken by mute sobs. No, not shaken, she's made me realize this, too. Who is there to cry about? Ourselves? As if we were created in His image, for Gods' sake? I was like a piece of rock that thinks it is an angel. Sometimes with her body – as far as I can tell, she fucks like an expert, consequently, when she initiated me she didn't take the easy way, she's fearless and wanton, and yet – sometimes with her body's absence, we swore chastity, but fell victim to the same contingency, she put an end to innocence, she left me to fend for myself, once and for all, she opened my eyes unto myself, this resplendent nothingness, with no comfort of any kind, no death, no immortality.

There's this woman. She loves me. She's got a wart on her back, a transition between a mole and a wart. I love her back. And having a hell of a time getting rid of her. When everything is set, and I am not just out of sorts and bitter, but also firmly resolved (at such times I think mostly of Effi Briest, she's my ideal), then softly, and as if by chance, as it were, she tells me that in the morning, as she lay on her back watching the clouds roll by the attic window, this grey swirling, it was like a prayer, a prayer for you. When I snap at her, but you don't even *believe* in God, she nods submissively. But she's not about to give in. She's holding the ace of spaces. It's as grey, she says, as your mother's eyes. As a result of which – sorry, Effi, old gal! – I simply can't say no to the swirling.

There's this woman. She's practically my guardian angel.
May the Good Lord watch over you, she whispers softly as
her wings flap and she lovingly nips me on the cheek.
Seeing how *I* can't (watch over myself). And she's off.
She laughs a great deal. Her ample gums and teeth show.
Nietzsche's horse, I once thought (she was making paprika
potatoes for twenty-five). She's suffering, it's written all over
her, try as she might to conceal it, but it's not something you
can conceal, because eventually you grow tired. She, too,
grows tired of the concealing, and then she stares, terrified,
into space. Her gleaming walnut-brown eyes are like a
supermodel's whose contract hasn't been renewed. For one
thing, she suffers from the burden of pain which has repeatedly settled on her shoulders through the course of her life.
At the age of seven, she was accidentally shut up in an
empty apartment for two days. Another time she woke to
a woolly caterpillar thick as my finger crawling up her
cheek, and she retched for several days afterwards. For thirty

175

years she has been nursing her paralysed mother, whose mind clears once in a great while and, when it does, she hates her daughter with unmitigated, clear-sighted hatred. Nor did she fare better as a mother; she lost seven children, each miscarried in the fifth month of her pregnancy, where-upon she adopted a little boy who robbed her blind, and so on. She has no luck with men either, yours truly included. Her stories are sad. That's one. For another, she suffers from life itself. She would still stare into space if all these things did not happen to her. She brings this into connection with God, not that she subordinates life to God in an attempt to escape from this vale of tears, no, it's just that she constantly feels her own lack of perfection, and this, she thinks, is not pleasing to God, which in turn makes her suffer, in short, the fact that it can't be otherwise, it can't very well be otherwise, seeing how she is a human being, while God is God. At times I think she's stark raving mad. She's not quite for this world, and this makes me feel ashamed. She washes with bio-soap and does not use deodorant, so at times she smells of sweat. From time to time she goes on a liquid diet, which affects her breath. When she sleeps, her face is beautiful. Once I caught her yelling, beside herself, into the phone (it wasn't me at the receiving end): I will put the semicolon where I damn well please! She also suffers because of me. I am helpless, and also a bit afraid of her. When she crosses the room, she leans over me. I pretend I'm asleep. She studies me. At such times I feel she hates me. But maybe I'm mistaken, I feel this, too. And since I sleep in the buff, my body feels that it is being watched. She does not move. May the Good Lord watch over you, she says as her wings flap and she lovingly nips me on the cheek. Seeing how I can't. And she's off.

There's this woman. She's finally warmed to me. We're mismatched. At times I find this annoying, at others I do not. When I find it annoying, I hate her, while she dotes on me with a passion I find shrill and unbearable. When this happens, her hips are wide, and she sways them like a hussy. When this happens, her lips are thick and her thinking is vulgar, her backside flat, her breath sour. What at other times passes for quick-wittedness is now merely felicitous and appropriate. What at other times passes for an astute assessment of the situation is now just selfish jockeying for position. The colourful becomes superficial, the tartness of her rare and expensive perfume smells, how shall I put it, like a cesspool, while her natural clownishness is so much hot air, her humour just clowning, her sweetness fawning, her severity rudeness, her high spirits a source of embarrassment, her low spirits sulking, her lively glance licentious, and so on, and so forth, anything, everything. When I do not find it annoying, then: I am crazy for her,

177

I pant like a puppy dog at the very sight of her, my knees shake and my palms sweat, and I regard myself as a child of Good Fortune that a woman like her condescends to notice me, while she: puts up with all this like a Sister of Charity. Her breasts are like an over-ripe teenager's, her hips as curvaceous as the Danube Bend (before the electric power plant).[21] Her crotch scorches the turf. Her skin is not blotched with liver spots, it is spectacular. Her lips have a life of their own, they tingle, they're not grainy, but pure taste, colour (fiery, up to no good, as usual). Her glance makes you tingle all over. Her gait is not a wriggle, but a wiggle. There is hardly a woman alive who can walk down a street like she can. Her walk creates a brand-new world ('*poetry in motion, walking by my si-ide!*'), city districts hover in the air, alleys, promenades, esplanades, balls, ballrooms, terraces, champagne-laden trays. She can stand as close to me, as close to my body, as no one else. I can stand for hours in front of the window, watching the lights of the city, with her behind me. She twines her body round my ribs. Pain, she whispers, is finite, my dear. Still, you must scream, *necesse est*. Scream with all your might. And it's not play-acting, it's the way of the world. She strikes, you scream. She strikes, you scream. If you do not scream, it could lead to trouble. Not only because she, not seeing the result of her labours, will be disappointed, morose, and this might prompt her to do 'unexpected' things, but because screaming conceals the pain, it comes between you and the pain, and you need that, yes, you need that if you expect

---

[21]The Communist governments of Hungary and neighbouring Czechoslovakia agreed to build an electric power plant at the most spectacular bend in the Danube, under the former palace of King Matthias at Visegrád, in order to supply part of southern Czechoslovakia with electricity. Though environmentalists, dissidents and the astute common folk alike were up in arms, nothing could be done until the 1990 elections.

to pass somehow, no matter how, beyond the endless expanse of the finite.

Or close.

There's this woman. She talks to me about men. We have an exchange of views. Right now it's some Eugene who is a gentleman from head to toe and is an expert on insurance mathematics. Oh, oh, oh, I just don't know!, she sobs, and buries her face in her hands. It's so fragile, all this, a pane of glass, that's what this whole thing is like; when I stand here – and she raises her hand in a tight little fist – life is beautiful, I take wing, and I am lovable. All you have to do is look at me – and that Eugene of yours, I bark – and you can see with your own eyes, I am swimming in a sea of bliss, and the world, too, revolves more easily. Does Eugene swim, too? She makes a face. Poor Eugene. I wouldn't like to be in his shoes. Sliding her fingers down my cheeks, deep in thought: what do you mean you wouldn't *like* to be? You *are*! And she's making a fist again, fixing her eyes on her tightly pressed fingers, see?, it moves just the slightest bit, and right away . . . She makes a face, I'm a piece of shit, a miserable piece of shit.

I try to change the course of the conversation, but we fare no better; time and again she ends up like poor Tsvetayeva,[22] mourning one of her lovers with another.

---

[22]Still the same frenetic, romantic Russian poet, (She Loves Me . . . 82)

she loves me...**90**

There's this woman. She loves me. She hates me. She loves me. She hates me. She's not even a woman. She's a man. He loves me. He hates me.

she loves me... **91**

There's this woman. Sometimes we don't see each other for years. What I mean is, quite *unexpectedly*, while I brush my teeth, twenty-eight years go by. Twenty-eight years are nothing to scoff at. Two such brushings of teeth can't even fit into a lifetime. Yet her face has not changed. She's got the same little-girl roses in her cheeks, her eyes are as bright as ever, her voice, too, is her customary voice. Even before this brushing of teeth I noticed a certain tendency in her to gain weight, and now it has happened, the body become flesh, not all of her, though, just her waist, and her bottom. Her bottom is pretty substantial. Not awesome, or anything; it doesn't dazzle you, it doesn't floor you, you don't gape. It's just big, disconsolately, tediously big. Twenty-eight years are twenty-eight years, no matter how you look at them. A while back, she broke her leg. She slipped on a turnip in the kitchen. Well, I'll be! When she shows me our son's picture, I let out a shriek, his features are so handsome and dignified, his blond locks tumbling about him like an angel's. Tadzio. The spitting image of Tadzio, I shout, bursting with pride. Every evening I kiss her clumsy little feet all over, a complicated fracture, her ankle twisted, like the Swede Brolin's during the football game against the Hungarians. I progress from the top down, sort of in reverse. (Oh, the eternal Donaueschingen,[23] the source and the origin, that's pretty damn straightforward I should think!) That Tadzio did the trick. Will you kindly accept the fact, Mother!, the boy had shouted. At which she fled to the kitchen, as it were, not watching her feet, asking for trouble. Will you accept the fact, Mother, queer!, and wham!, there went her ankle, right under her. We stand by him, though. We even invited his friend for Christmas who, however, declined. What tact. Sometimes I think about the question of inheritance, how it will be, *what* will be in place of grandchildren, and so forth. I also brush my teeth every night.

---

[23]A town in the Black Forest region of Germany where two small streams unite to form the River Danube.

she Loves me... **92**

There's this woman. She loves me. On the other hand, she doesn't know the meaning of hate. Which, of course, is not the same as loving. Goethe. She's the spitting image of Goethe. They're as alike as two eggs. Her forehead, her hair, her eyes, the hollows around her eyes. I keep on telling her, but she won't listen. She refuses to look at a picture of Goethe. What are you afraid of? She won't tell me, she presses her lips tightly together, she won't look, anywhere. Would you rather it was Kleist? She shrugs. She's never even heard of Kleist, I bet. Or just the barest wind of him. A breeze. A breath. A whiff. She's not what you'd call highly educated, though she's no dummy either. She's a refined intellectual who has lived alone time and time again; what I mean is, she has withdrawn, so she could be alone. She spends a lot of time thinking, that's what has refined her. She can hardly find words for this, but this doesn't put a limit on her refinement, which in turns is immediately apparent, obvious, even though she hasn't got a pushy bone in her body. I shouldn't be loath to use the word wisdom, wise, yes, she is wise and refined. And works very hard. She's been working hard for ages. She works like a robot. Or more like an animal. I watch her from a distance. She huffs and puffs, her cheeks are red, her wide forehead covered with beads of perspiration. When I talk to her she listens intently, her head inclined to the side, and there is no telling, is she smiling, or what. Johann Wolfgang, I mumble, as she chastely runs her fingers through my hair.

she loves me...**93**

           There's this man. He loves me. He loves me tender, he loves me true. Just like a woman. I had my suspicions, of course, but I never gave it much thought. I thought about it less than you'd expect, the reasons for which will have to remain shrouded in mystery. Anyway, yesterday I received the following letter from him:

My dear friend,

I am writing you this letter from a box-size room in Frankfurt. A box that I now call my home. *Schachtel.* Everything here is box-like, *Schachtel*, my life included. The door is closed, I can't see out of the window, each one is covered by repulsive Venetian blinds, plastic, and behind them, fire walls, Manhattan, as the local joke would have it. I was a loner all my life, but never have I experienced solitude as keenly as now, nor the fact that I am at other people's mercy. But maybe just a stranger. I hate this city. It is full of well-dressed people with bad faces. Anything might happen in this place, and there is no one I could count on.

I know that this letter will surprise you, and perhaps also the fact that I am so forward with you; I have never been this familiar with you, even in my thoughts. Never. I would never have written this letter back home, I wouldn't have dared, you were too close, and I was always with you anyway, always; there was no 'need and opportunity' for me to do so. But now I feel that I cannot go on without you. I want you to talk to me, to speak to me, with authentic, human words.

Without the new distance between us I would never have admitted, not even to myself, what I know so well, what I already knew and will continue to know ... namely, that I need you, I need your thoughts, your feelings, your friendship. What is there to prevent us working together? I brought your picture along. It is not alive. It does not speak to me. It is just so much glossy paper that I stroke in vain. It doesn't do the trick.

Consider, please, that I am writing a confession; this solitude can be shared only with you. Sympathy from any other quarter would be degrading. I realize that for some mysterious reason I cannot fathom, which is very real all the same, I have no right to love, I must love you only with my soul; my body must not know, and indeed does not know, what love is. Until now I even doubted whether I could love at all. Well, I can. I can, I can. You are the only real thing in my life. Where would I run from you? Now that I have said it, I am happy, and I am free, too, at last, but this freedom does not give me any rights, nor does it put you under obligation. Be liberal-minded, my dear, don't be embarrassed or withdrawn. I repeat: I love you. See? My pen falters; it is difficult, even writing it. I have waited ten years to do so.

You must know, I want you to know, I cannot lose

you. (. . .) It is night now, but I know that tomorrow I will mail this letter.

I am reading it for the tenth time. I know it by heart. My hand shakes. I am apprehensive and jubilant. Tomorrow I will be neither apprehensive, nor jubilant. But I will know the letter inside and out. Backwards and forwards. By the letter. By the book.

she loves me...**94**

There's this woman. She loves me. She never gasps for breath. Why not? It's good with her, except she doesn't gasp for breath. Right now this bothers me more than anything in the world, this silence, this lack of sound in which only *I* am heard, the yelping of my passion reaching for the sky.

There's this woman. She hates me. She loves me, except she's as scared of my prick as the devil is of incense. It frightens her half to death, her courage fails her, yes, indeed; she clasps her hands together, she screams and jumps on top of the table as if there was a mouse in the room. This is especially awkward when we have company and the table is laid for supper. It is always laid beautifully, by the way, with lots of taste and invention; sometimes a long gourd runner meanders its way among the plates, at other times a yard-long leek stalk splits the table in two, like a sword. Since it is mostly our friends dining with us, they're very understanding. They wait around a while, then seeing that the Holy Ghost is turning a cartwheel in her, they get their act together and leave, often taking our kids with them, and go to a nearby restaurant for dinner. Once we are alone, I try to calm her down, but she calms down only when the mouse is back in its hole. But sometimes she's so scared, even this doesn't do the trick. Anyway, until our guests return, we nibble, so it shouldn't go to waste. If we have no guests and we're not preparing a big dinner, there's less fuss; on the other hand, dinner is served with a slight delay.

There's this woman. She hates me. She doesn't know the meaning of modesty, which I accept, though I don't encourage it. In company, I let her feel me up. Get some action on the sly. Under the table, she'll slide the naked sole of her foot, made naked for the occasion, up and down my leg. Given half a chance, she'll playfully jam her knee into my groin. Or bite my neck. I don't look her in the eye. I feel her right back, unseeing, I pet, I paw. We chit-chat, yes, that's the right expression. She can't get a grip on herself. If I'm within fifty yards of her, she can't get a grip on herself. But I'd rather spare myself the details, if you don't mind. If I so much as stroke her neck, her body explodes. She often takes me to the train by car, so I can get into town faster, and if I stroke her neck then, she promptly stops by the roadside (provided there are no signs to the contrary), and makes a diving header for my groin. She usually can't manage the zipper, so I have to help, but I fumble a bit myself. She reassures me every time how much she loves me, in her mouth, so to speak, but to me she sounds like her feelings are hurt. At least, that's how I feel. I'd make the train a whole lot faster on foot.

she loves me... **97**

There's this woman. She loves me. She loves me less and less, and wants me more and more. When I pressed her up against the wall, she opened of her own accord. Now I don't even have to stir, and right away, I'm in. Even when I reach for the salt, I end up inside her. When we take the tram, we punch our tickets together. When I inhale, I must filch the air from between her lips. I even found her eye-tooth in my mouth one day. I am a shaman. I find it more and more difficult to find me a name. I haven't even got my own toothbrush any more.